PAINT

PAINT

JENNIFER DANCE

DUNDURN
TORONTO

Editor: Allison Hirst
Interior Design: Colleen Wormald
Cover Design: Laura Boyle
Printer: Webcom

Library and Archives Canada Cataloguing in Publication
Dance, Jennifer, author
        Paint / Jennifer Dance.

Issued in print and electronic formats.
ISBN 978-1-4597-2868-4 (pbk.).--ISBN 978-1-4597-2869-1 (pdf).--
ISBN 978-1-4597-2870-7 (epub)

        1. Horses--Juvenile fiction. 2. Great Plains--History--Juvenile
fiction. I. Title.

PS8607.A548P35 2015   jC813'.6   C2014-904258-2   C2014-904259-0

1   2   3   4   5   19   18   17   16   15

Conseil des Arts du Canada   Canada Council for the Arts   Canadä   ONTARIO ARTS COUNCIL CONSEIL DES ARTS DE L'ONTARIO an Ontario government agency un organisme du gouvernement de l'Ontario

We acknowledge the support of the **Canada Council for the Arts** and the **Ontario Arts Council** for our publishing program. We also acknowledge the financial support of the **Government of Canada** through the **Canada Book Fund** and **Livres Canada Books**, and the **Government of Ontario** through the **Ontario Book Publishing Tax Credit** and the **Ontario Media Development Corporation**.

Care has been taken to trace the ownership of copyright material used in this book. The author and the publisher welcome any information enabling them to rectify any references or credits in subsequent editions.

J. Kirk Howard, President

The publisher is not responsible for websites or their content unless they are owned by the publisher.

Printed and bound in Canada.

VISIT US AT
Dundurn.com | *@dundurnpress* | *Facebook.com/dundurnpress* | *Pinterest.com/dundurnpress*

Dundurn
3 Church Street, Suite 500
Toronto, Ontario, Canada
M5E 1M2

To the special horses who have shared my life: Hollyhock, Freddy, Marty, Cruise, Silken, and Whisper. These horses taught me so much. Without them I would never have been able to write this story.

PROLOGUE
1895

The old mare sensed that something was wrong. She was agitated. In her youth she would have snorted and galloped around the paddock with her tail held high, but with age she had become slower, less excitable. Even so, her body trembled and she couldn't settle down to graze. Not that there was much to graze on. The grass had gone, and she had eaten most of the weeds in the paddock, except for the thistles. She would have to be starving before risking a pricked lip. And she wasn't starving, not quite.

She wandered across the field, pawing occasionally at the bare ground, asking it to yield something edible. She dug up some grass roots. Curling back her lips, she grasped the tuft with her front teeth, tossed her head to dislodge the clods of earth, then chewed, thoughtfully, slowly, her few remaining molars grinding against the grit.

The air was changing now. She could feel the hair on her back beginning to rise. She paced back and forth in front of the gate, her agitation building, her heart rate increasing. Everything inside her was responding to a message from that deep and ancient part of her brain that told her to bolt, to escape, because her life was in danger. But she couldn't get away. She was fenced in.

Frantic, she pushed against the gate, then reached to mouth the latch. But even before her damp nose touched the metal, a spark flew across the charged air. It snapped and crackled, biting her as if she'd been stung by wasps. She jumped back, startled and perplexed. There were no wasps. No lightning. No thunder. No rain. Not even a nearby cowhand cracking his whip.

Something hit the ground with a thump, not far from her nose. She jumped sideways, then bolted away at full gallop.

After a few strides she realized that the predator wasn't chasing her, so she stopped to take stock of the situation. It was neither an eagle nor a wolf, just a small bird. It had no markings, nothing to make it out of the ordinary. But the horse knew there was something extraordinary in the way the creature came to be at her feet. Something was wrong, but she didn't know what. Birds didn't fall from the sky. They fluttered down, or glided on outstretched wings. They didn't hit the dirt so hard that they bounced.

From a safe distance the old mare's curiosity got the better of her fear. She stretched her neck down and sniffed. The aroma of grass and seed made her braver. The creature wasn't a predator. Predators smelled of meat. Gingerly she walked toward it, snorting and blowing, bobbing her head, the bird's unusual presence still warning her to be wary. It lay still, dust settling on its unblinking eye. Suddenly it gasped, and the mare spun away. But the downy breast didn't rise again. After a few seconds the old horse was brave enough to touch a feather with her whiskers. She knew then that the spirit of life had left the creature.

Another bird fell not far from her, hitting the parched earth with an equally alarming thump that sent a puff of dust into the air. Again, the horse shied away, dancing for a moment in the shadows that flickered over her back. The moving patterns of light and dark told her that a flock of birds was overhead. Soon they blotted out the burning sun, leaving the horse in total shade. More birds fell from the sky like hailstones. She raised her tail and pranced away from them into the bright sunlight on the edge of the paddock.

Then suddenly the flock was gone.

The air stilled. But not for long.

The dust storm slammed into her.

There was no shelter for the old horse. She turned her rump to the wind, arched her back, lowered her head, and braced against the onslaught.

Her black-and-white markings vanished under a coat of sand.

CHAPTER ONE

1870

The mustangs were barely visible as they loped across the rolling plain, their multicoloured spots and smudges melding with the earth and rocks, their streaming manes and tails masquerading as tall grasses blowing in the constant prairie breeze.

Despite the vast open grassland around them, the horses were bunched up, pressing into one another, head to flank, nose to tail. Yearlings gambolled, bursting ahead of their mothers, trying to goad them into play, but most of the mares were heavy with foal and couldn't be provoked. A slow lope was all they could manage.

The boss mare was taking the herd back to the place where most of them had been born, an area of scrubby woodland where mustangs could hold the wolves at bay, a place where the newborns would have a better chance of survival than on the open plain. But something was wrong, and had been for a while. Neither the gentle lope nor the warm sun was reason for the leader of the herd to be sweating so profusely. She stopped and flung her head back to nip at her flank. Then she kicked up at her belly with a hind leg. The feelings weren't new to her; she had foaled many times before, but this time it was different. The feelings were lasting too long.

She groaned and lowered herself to the ground, stretching out on her side, her tail swishing furiously, but it didn't seem to help, so she heaved herself up and kicked at her belly again. The other horses stopped and waited with her, anxiously snatching mouthfuls of grass here and there. The labouring mare heaved herself up and down many times before she wearied and lay quietly in the grass. Still, the herd waited.

The mare's yearling colt stayed close, nudging and licking her. The others sniffed the air. The scent of birth made them anxious. Countless generations of wild ancestry had taught the horses that birth odour attracted their most feared predator: wolves. All of the horses knew they should be moving on, seeking safety. Their legs itched to run. But their leader still had power over them. She thrashed her head occasionally as if to let them know she was still living, still dominant, still in charge.

Another odour tinged the air, too: humans. It was a smell that demanded the wild horses flee. But the herd was leaderless. Several of the mustangs made brief sorties, trotting boldly away before returning with wide eyes, anxiety pinching their lips and tightening their nostrils.

Suddenly an older mare walked purposefully away from the herd and didn't look back. Immediately, many of the horses followed her, but some stayed, remaining loyal to their helpless leader for just a few more minutes. Then their survival instinct kicked in, and they loped after the others. The yearling colt was the last to leave, but eventually he, too, spun on his haunches, whisked his half-grown tail over his back, and galloped after the herd.

The boy known as Noisy Horse was in his twelfth summer when he found the painted mustang. He had not noticed the wild horses loping across the prairie, nor had he seen the herd anxiously waiting for nature to take its course. He had not even seen the pricked ears of his family's horses as they stared into the distance, trying to catch a glimpse of their wild cousins. It was the raucous distant cries of ravens that caught his attention. They were circling in the sky, some way off from the tipis. Noisy Horse knew it meant that a creature was dying out on the plain, so he jogged off to investigate.

The mare was easy to spot, a black-and-white mound in the short grass, directly under the flight path of the big black birds. She was on her side, as if she was sleeping, stretched out in the sun. The boy approached gently, unsure if she was alive or dead, half expecting her to startle and jump to her feet, yet knowing she would not let him get this close if she was still alive. When he saw her eyes, he knew for sure. The light in them had gone.

The wolves had not yet found her, but Noisy Horse suspected that it would not be long. The ravens were calling for them, needing the carnivores to rip open the carcass and serve the scavenging birds their meal.

It was only as he turned to leave that Noisy Horse saw the newborn filly, hidden in a clump of taller grass. She was painted like her mother, but smoky grey and white. And also like her mother, she lay flat on her side. But she was not dead. The boy could see her nostrils twitching. As he moved closer, she tried to scramble up, but her legs didn't hold her for more than a second before she collapsed to the ground. Noisy Horse wanted to help, to steady her, to stroke his fingers across her soft new coat, but he held back, sensing that he would frighten her. Instead he watched, spellbound.

She was mostly grey, but was splattered with white splotches, drips, and speckles. Her long ears were solid grey, as was her head, except for a white blaze that dashed around one eye then coursed down her dished nose like a waterfall, splashing her dark nostrils with white spray.

She was the most beautiful foal he had ever seen. But he was terrified by how fragile she was. All of his life had been spent with horses. His father was the trainer of the band's herd. Yet the boy didn't know what to do. He knew exactly what his father would say, though: *Son, there's nothing we can do. She needs her mother's milk, especially the first milk. Without that, she will die.*

In his imagination the boy could see his father's shoulders rise and fall in a defeated sigh. *My son, you must accept that death will soon visit her. It is not wise to get your hopes high.*

But the boy's hopes *were* high. He hoped that the painted mare had lived long enough for the foal to drink the first milk. And he hoped that if he took the young one home, Swift, his father's favourite mare, might mother her. He knew that mares, even bereaved ones like Swift, usually turned on orphans, driving them away, refusing to give them life. Yet he hoped.

He wondered if he should leave the filly alone and run back to the village to fetch his father; but the ravens were starting to attack him, trying to drive him away from the mare's carcass. They were hungry, and getting more so with every passing moment. They'd been calling the wolves for some time now, and Noisy Horse knew that it wouldn't be long before the pack arrived. He couldn't risk leaving the little filly alone. Stooping, he picked her up and settled her across his shoulders, her front legs down one side of his chest, her hind legs down the other. She was heavier than he imagined, but she didn't struggle and that made it easier. Clutching all four hooves in his hands, he started for home.

The conversation with his father went nothing like Noisy Horse had expected. Touch the Sky was pleased that his son had brought the foal home, saying that it might be the perfect solution to two sad events, the pairing of an orphaned foal and a bereaved mare.

Noisy Horse sank to one knee and twisted his shoulders, allowing the newborn to slip off into the grass. The mare came over and sniffed, then swung around and kicked out at the orphan. But Touch the Sky was ready for her. He'd seen this behaviour before. He charged at the mare with arms raised above his head, hands open and fingers curled like claws. Swift backed off and watched him from afar.

Touch the Sky took his skinning knife from his belt. "Keep Swift away from the foal for a while. I'll be back soon."

Under normal circumstances Noisy Horse would have been intimidated by the aggression that the mare had just displayed, but today he felt brave. Defending the helpless foal had turned him into a fighter. He was ready to pounce like a wolf, just as his father had done. He straddled the newborn, squared his body up to the mare, made himself as big as he could, and with arms raised and hands in claws, he stared fiercely at Swift. She hung her head and seemed repentant.

Touch the Sky wasn't gone for long. He returned with the skin of Swift's stillborn colt. Noisy Horse lifted the orphan to her feet, supporting her while Touch the Sky draped the skin over her back and fastened it with rawhide strips. The painted filly had taken on the identity of a brown colt.

"If this doesn't work, then nothing will," Touch the Sky said.

The boy let go of the foal. She slumped to the ground. Swift soon became curious, sniffing the air, extending her head and curling back her top lip to inhale more of the scent. Then she approached.

Father and son watched anxiously. The mare tentatively licked the dead colt's skin. She recognized the odour and taste of her own offspring. Nickering softly, she pushed her nose under the two tails, one fuzzy brown, the other fuzzy grey, absorbing the scent of both foals and making them her own. Then she started licking frantically.

Touch the Sky and Noisy Horse looked at each other and beamed.

Swift's tongue moved to the dished face that poked out from the brown skin, then to the delicately curved grey ears, and the spindly legs that were folded neatly under her.

The foal perked up and struggled to stand. With a nudge from the mare, she was on her feet, weaving a little, but wobbling toward the scent of the milk that was already dripping from the mare's udder. Noisy Horse held his breath as the foal's lips groped around. The sorrel mare shifted her body, trying to help, and finally the foal found what she was looking for. Father and son breathed a sigh of relief.

"How long will she wear the skin?" Noisy Horse asked.

"Not long. I'll cut off a chunk tomorrow. Then another piece the next day. By then I'm sure Swift will be accustomed to the little filly's smell."

Touch the Sky rested his hand on his son's shoulder. "Sometimes things work out just perfectly, don't they?"

CHAPTER TWO

From the moment his son entered the world, Touch the Sky had hoped that the boy would share his passion for horses. The child needed no encouragement! He was only three when his mother gave him the nickname Noisy Horse, because he was forever cantering between the tipis, tossing his head and neighing loudly. Now that he was older, the boy had stopped doing such childish things, but his heart still belonged to horses and the nickname stuck. It suited him.

Noisy Horse was allowed to ride most of the ponies in the herd, but he didn't have his own special mount, like his father did, or like his uncles and grandfather. Touch the Sky had Swift, the one he loved more than any other, the one he rode in the buffalo hunt. They trusted each other. They had to, because buffalo hunting was very dangerous. A horse and rider could be gored or trampled. The life of both depended on mutual trust.

Touch the Sky wanted that same kind of partnership for Noisy Horse. For a long time he'd hoped that one of Swift's foals would become the special horse for his son, but Swift's latest foal had died and Touch the Sky's hopes had been dashed. Watching the painted orphan sniff the boy's hand, and seeing wonder spread across his face, Touch the Sky felt sure that the pair would be perfect for each other.

Touch the Sky spoke softly to the filly. "If you have half the courage, and speed, and wisdom of your new mother, you will one day be a great horse. But not yet. Now you must eat, and grow, and eat some more. And you must learn from Swift. She is a good mother and a good horse. You must learn from the others in the herd, too. They will teach you how to be a horse. Then, when you have seen two or three summers, my son will show you the ways of our people. And you will become a great buffalo-runner. With him on your back, you will be more than a painted horse. He will put courage into your heart. Two will be as one."

The boy's jaw dropped. He was stunned by his father's words. The foal was to be his!

"And you, my son," Touch the Sky continued, "when you ride this painted horse, you will be more than a man. You will have wings on your feet."

Noisy Horse felt as if his heart might burst.

"So now you have to give your new friend a name," Touch the Sky said.

The boy had already decided on that. "Her name is Paint."

🐎

Noisy Horse spent most of his free time with Paint, rushing through his chores to be at her side. The first thing he had to learn, however, was how to deal with the foal's adoptive mother. Swift had become so protective of the newborn that she flattened her ears against her head whenever Noisy Horse approached the foal. The boy learned to glare at Swift with a confident stance, determined not to be intimidated, even though his stomach was churning. The mare soon agreed to share the filly with Noisy Horse.

Touch the Sky knew the benefit of handling horses when they were young, so he encouraged his son to stroke Paint all over, finding the places that she liked best. She would lean her weight into the boy when he scratched her neck close to the base of her ears. And she would poke her nose to the sky, grunting, when he rubbed her chest.

Paint was only a few weeks old when father and son slipped a leather loop over her head, tying it fast. The filly didn't like the feeling and shook her head from side to side, then rubbed her face against Swift's ribs. But the halter didn't come off, and soon Paint forgot it was even there. But when Noisy Horse tugged at the rope, expecting to lead her, she dug in her hooves and stood firm. The boy held the rope taut. Paint panicked, almost throwing herself to the ground to escape the pressure on her head.

"Stop!" Touch the Sky ordered. "She'll hurt herself that way! You'll never succeed with brute force. The horse will always win when it comes to strength." He chuckled. "I mean a proper horse, not a little scrap like this one!"

As soon as the boy let the rope go slack, Paint relaxed. She opened her mouth and clacked her teeth.

"See, that means she's thinking about things."

"What is she thinking?"

"She says that she is just a baby and she wants to please you," Touch the Sky replied. "Next time, pull gently to the side, not straight ahead. That way she'll be off balance and it's easier to make her move."

Sure enough, with a slight sideways tug, the foal moved a few steps toward the boy.

🐎

Noisy Horse was expected to take his turn guarding the herd, watching for wild stallions that might try to steal away the mares, or wolves that might attack the foals. When he was younger, he and his friends also had to watch for neighbouring bands and tribes that might steal horses. Sometimes it was a fun game that the braves played, but other times it was with serious intent. Recently, however, the tribal games and wars had ceased. The mighty Red Cloud had persuaded Lakota, Cheyenne, and Arapaho to set aside their squabbles and unify against the common enemy: the white man.

Noisy Horse had never seen a white man, but he had listened to the talk of the elders as they sat around the fires. And he well remembered the day when several warriors had ridden away to join Red Cloud. At the time, he didn't understand why they were leaving, but now he knew. They went to protest against the white man's Bozeman Trail and to fight the soldiers and settlers who were following the trail right through the heart of their traditional territory.

Later, the elders had proudly told the story of the *Battle of the Hundred Slain,* praising the band's warriors who had ridden as decoys with Chief Crazy Horse. They had bravely lured the soldiers into an ambush, allowing the unified Arapaho, Cheyenne, and Lakota tribes to kill all of the soldiers. What's more, it was American Horse, one of their own, who had slain the leader of the troops. Noisy Horse felt proud that he, too, carried the horse medicine.

For Noisy Horse, these things had happened in another world, far from his. Unconcerned, he watched the horses graze. Even wolf attacks happened so rarely that he was able to spend most of the time studying Paint. At first Swift was protective of her, chasing off curious horses by baring her teeth and charging. But, as with most new mothers, she became less protective as Paint became more rambunctious, and soon Paint's growing curiosity started leading her astray. Her coat became marred by missing tufts of fluffy hair, and sometimes her skin was broken by teeth marks. Tika, the herd's leader, was the culprit. Noisy Horse didn't understand why the blue roan mare was so aggressive toward the little filly.

PAINT

Touch the Sky sat with Noisy Horse one day, father and son enjoying the late-day sunshine that glinted off of the creek, filling the plain with brilliant silver light. Tika suddenly charged at Paint, driving her away. She then calmly began grazing where Paint had just been eating. Noisy Horse was outraged. "Why did she do that? There's grass everywhere! Why does she need those few blades? She's being so mean!"

"It's not about the grass," Touch the Sky replied. "It's about who's in charge. Tika has to show Paint that she is boss. She will keep Paint there on the edge of the herd as punishment for not obeying quickly."

"What kind of punishment is that? Paint is not far away. She can still see the others and hear them."

"Instinct tells an exiled horse that he will be the first one to be eaten by wolves," Touch the Sky explained. "Mares always keep the young ones on the inside of the group to protect them from predators. Right now, all of Paint's senses are telling her to get back to the safety of the herd. But Tika won't let her."

"How can you tell?" Noisy Horse asked.

"From the way she stands. See how she just raised her head and glared at Paint? And see how Paint is clacking her teeth. She's saying please let me back in. I've learned my lesson."

Even before Touch the Sky had finished the sentence, Tika softened her gaze, let her ears flop sideways, and turned away from Paint, as if no longer interested. The filly quickly read Tika's body

23

language and rejoined the herd, greeting Swift as if she had been away for days.

"Soon your filly will learn to read Tika's warning signs — the flattened ears, or the tossed head — then she won't have to use her teeth."

"But why must Tika be so bossy?"

"A herd always has a boss mare," Touch the Sky explained. "She protects them from danger."

"But she's biting and kicking them!"

"She is teaching them obedience. They must do as she says immediately. In the wild their lives depend on it. She makes the hard decisions for them, about where to go for food and water and shelter. And she is constantly alert for danger, telling them when to run for their lives. Once they have learned to be obedient and respectful, they can relax, knowing that she will keep them safe."

"But how do they know she will keep them safe?"

Touch the Sky took some time searching for an answer. "They know ... based on experience. They obey her because they trust her, because she is a worthy leader. Once a boss mare is too old, or too weak, the horses no longer follow her. If she lets them down, they choose a new leader, one who is more trustworthy."

Paint had finished greeting the other horses and was now using her baby teeth to nibble the grass. Tika approached from the rear, pinning her ears and stretching her neck forward. Paint tucked her fluffy tail and scooted away. Tika ate the grass where Paint had been.

"See!" Touch the Sky said, grinning broadly. "Your little filly is learning."

Paint was a leggy yearling. Her soft grey-and-white baby fluff had been replaced with a sleek black-and-white coat, and her black tail was half grown. She was learning how to be a horse, and how to submit to the will of others in the herd. But she was less respectful of the boy. He was not growing as quickly as she was. And he was not as strong. She was becoming pushy with him.

Touch the Sky knew that a pushy yearling would turn into a disrespectful two-year-old, and ultimately a dangerous horse. He needed to show his son how to stop Paint's bad behaviour.

Tying a rope to her halter, he asked Noisy Horse to lead Paint away from Swift. There was a strong attachment between the filly and her adoptive mother. Paint dug in her heels and reared up. Noisy Horse shook the rope repeatedly in her face. It sent waves of irritation to her head and she came back to all fours and ran backward, trying to escape from the sensation. Noisy Horse kept shaking until she was a full rope-length away from him.

"Now hold her there with your eyes and your body," Touch the Sky instructed.

"How?" Noisy Horse asked.

"Pretend you are Tika!"

Noisy Horse squared himself up to Paint, made

himself as tall as possible, and glared at her with all the determination he could muster.

"Don't let her move closer to you!" Touch the Sky ordered. "If she steps forward, wiggle the rope again and drive her back. Remember, horses hate being alone."

Paint took a step toward the boy. He shook the rope until she stepped back again.

"She's on her own out there at the end of the rope," Touch the Sky said. "She's getting lonely. She's feeling vulnerable, just as when Tika drives her out of the herd. Any moment now she'll want to come back to you, just like she always wants to go back to the herd. She needs to be close to you. She wants to be part of *your* herd! But it has to be when *you* let her. Because *you* are the boss."

Paint lowered her head and chewed as if there was food in her mouth.

"That's what I was waiting for!" Touch the Sky exclaimed. "She's submitting to you as leader. "Lower you gaze, relax your body, and smile!"

Paint walked right up to Noisy Horse then. He rubbed her forehead, telling her how clever she was.

"She can't tell I'm smiling, can she?" Noisy Horse asked.

"Of course, she can," Touch the Sky replied. "Horses have big eyes that are set on the sides of their heads so they can see all around. They see many things that we cannot see. How could Paint miss that big, broad grin on your face?"

PAINT

As Paint matured, it was obvious to Touch the Sky that she was not, by nature, a submissive horse. Time and again she challenged Noisy Horse. Touch the Sky took the time to sit with his son, watching how the horses interacted in the herd. He hoped to teach the boy how to act and think like a boss horse. He believed this was the only way that Noisy Horse could become Paint's leader.

"See how they speak to each other," he advised.

"They don't speak to each other," Noisy Horse said.

"Of course they do! They say lots of things, but not with words like ours. They speak with body language."

Gradually the boy saw what his father meant. But he still didn't understand why Touch the Sky was so insistent about small things, such as making Paint walk behind him instead of in front.

"What difference does it make if she has her nose in front of me, so long as she's going my way?" he asked.

"The herd leader leads! The submissive horses follow. There can be only one leader. When a horse pushes in front of the herd leader, he is trying to be boss. We must act just like the leader, and put him back in his place. If a horse even thinks about bossing us around we must stop him, or he will hurt us."

So with time, Noisy Horse learned to think and act like a horse. He cared for Paint and watched out for her, like the boss mare; and also like the boss, he refused to tolerate disrespect. Once, when he brought her food, she pushed him away so she could start eating. He leaped in the air, waving his hands. She stepped back in alarm. But she soon forgot the lesson. The next time she pushed him, he reacted even more strongly. He frightened her so much with his jumping and waving that she started to run away from him. He chased her, just like Tika, driving her away from him. He chased her long after she wanted to stop and submit to his leadership. He chased her until they were both puffing. Even then he kept her away with a glare. She licked and chewed, telling him that she had learned the lesson. And she had. She never pushed Noisy Horse again.

CHAPTER THREE

As far back as he could remember, Noisy Horse had taken part in the buffalo hunt. While still in a cradleboard, he had watched the women skin the buffalo and cut up the meat. As a small boy, he had scoured low bushes with the other children, picking berries and herbs to use as seasoning for the meat and fat. Child-sized hands were perfect for packing the mixture into buffalo-hide bags. As he grew older he had stoked the fires, keeping them burning low with just the right amount of sun-dried buffalo dung to smoke and dry both the meat and the skins.

But now Noisy Horse was stronger than the women in the band and that gave him a new status in the buffalo hunt. One of his jobs was to load and unload the heavy pieces of buffalo meat into the horse-drags.

Two-year-old Paint was still too young to be ridden, but Noisy Horse saw no reason why she shouldn't help him pull meat from the kill site to the camp. Touch the Sky had promised to accustom the horse to the drag, but the boy was impatient to be a man. He wanted to show his father he could do it alone.

Paint stood quietly while he attached two long poles, one on either flank, fastening the leading edges around her chest with a hide collar. She turned her head from side to side, keeping a keen eye on the blind spot right behind her tail, where Noisy Horse was tying a buffalo hide between the poles. When he started loading bags of fresh meat onto the hide, her heart started to race, instinct warning her that death was too close for comfort. Noisy Horse was too preoccupied to notice the filly's crinkled nostrils, her tight lips, or her tense muscles. With the drag filled, he clucked at her from behind, urging her forward. She tried to respond, but was restrained by the load, so she stopped dead. Noisy Horse clicked and clucked to no avail, so he smacked her rump.

The unexpected slap propelled her forward, yanking the rein from the boy's hand. But the load chased her! It smelled of blood and freshly killed meat, and was undoubtedly a predator. She bolted away, head up, eyes wide. But as fast as she galloped, she couldn't outrun the animal on her tail. Nature had equipped Paint with speed, agility, and stamina to outrun many predators, but today speed wasn't helping. She kicked out while she ran, but the animal chasing her didn't retreat. Instead, it stayed a short distance away, just out of striking range. With heaving chest, she finally stopped. Her unknown pursuer stood its ground, threatening to nip her hind legs. Suddenly Paint changed from victim to attacker. She turned to strike out with her forelegs, prepared to rear and crush the creature under her flailing hooves. The pole snapped with a crack that sent a new surge of fear through her. She bolted across the prairie and didn't stop until all of the meat had bounced from the drag and both poles were in pieces. With the predator no longer on her tail, she rested, huffing, licking and chewing thoughtfully until Noisy Horse caught up with her. He spoke gently, led her back home, and with new poles he tried again. Paint soon learned that with the boy nearby, the predator that followed so close to her hind hooves would not hurt her.

She wasn't able to see the proud smile on the boy's face when Touch the Sky watched them dragging meat back to camp the first time, but the boy's fingers massaged her withers and that made her feel good.

Paint and Noisy Horse spent three summers together. They were calm in each other's company. But on this day Noisy Horse found it impossible to be calm. He had waited so long to ride Paint that he could barely contain his excitement. He climbed onto a rock, intending to slide gently across onto her back, but Paint sensed his tension, and she fidgeted and danced, moving away from his weight, side-stepping so that he slithered to the ground.

"I'll bring Swift alongside," Touch the Sky suggested.

With the older mare blocking her, Paint allowed the boy to climb onto her back for the first time. Her heart raced. Noisy Horse could feel it through his legs. He felt her coil up under him, about to explode into motion.

"She's going to bolt!" he said.

"Talk to her, let her know that you are not a wolf," Touch the Sky advised.

"She knows I'm not a wolf!" Noisy Horse protested, nervousness tingeing his voice.

"Calm yourself, son," Touch the Sky continued. "If you are calm, it will help her to overcome her fear."

Noisy Horse took a deep breath and tried to relax.

"And as for thinking that you are a wolf," Touch the Sky continued, his voice low and serene, "that's exactly what she thinks! When you stand at her side she has no fear of you, but right now, you are like a wolf that has jumped on her back to kill her."

Noisy Horse sat quietly, scratching Paint's withers with his fingers, as he had done so many times when he stood beside her on the ground. He kept his voice to a soft murmur. Eventually Paint's racing heart slowed and her tense muscles relaxed.

During that first ride, whenever Swift changed direction, Paint changed direction along with her. When Swift slowed or stopped, Paint did, too. But on the second ride, Noisy Horse began to act differently. He pressed one of his legs against her side. She moved away from the uncomfortable pressure, stepping sideways, just as she had always moved away from the nudges and nips of the dominant horses in the herd. And as with the nudges and nips, the pressure stopped as soon as she obeyed.

He squeezed both legs around Paint's chest. She ignored him, not understanding his request. Noisy Horse reached back toward her tail and lightly smacked her rump. She surged forward, as she would have from one of Tika's nips. Noisy Horse got left behind. His legs tightened around her slippery rib-cage, and his hands flailed, trying to clutch a lock of her flying mane.

This was another new sensation for Paint — and she didn't like it. She bolted. Suddenly Noisy Horse was on the ground, and Paint was galloping free, reins dragging. Noisy Horse stood and dusted himself off as Paint trotted back to them. They all walked back to the rock and started the process over again.

CHAPTER FOUR

Touch the Sky was worried about his son. Noisy Horse was in his fifteenth summer, the time when young men learn to be buffalo hunters. The boy was keen to learn; too keen, Touch the Sky thought. He knew how easily a horse could get gored by a spooked buffalo. He had seen both horses and men die.

Touch the Sky felt conflicted. He wanted to protect his son, but he also knew that he had to allow the boy to become a man. The elders would soon need to depend on the younger generation. Without them, the women and children would starve, the whole tribe would die. There was an even bigger worry that troubled Touch the Sky, filling his heart with both pride and anxiety in equal measure; Noisy Horse would soon become a warrior.

In times gone by, the Oglála Lakota had fought, not to defend or gain new territory, but to prove their courage. Wars against the Cheyenne, the Arapaho, the Kiowa, and the Comanche were rarely fights to the death. Villages and property were seldom harmed. Touch the Sky could still feel the excitement of pouncing on his foe and claiming victory with a light touch to the chest. And he could still recall the excitement of stealing a horse, knowing full well that its owner would scheme and plot to steal it back. But times had changed. Brave young men were leaving their family bands and going far away to fight the soldiers and the settlers. It seemed to Touch the Sky that many warriors did not return.

The inner musings of his father's mind were of no concern to Noisy Horse. It was the upcoming buffalo hunt that consumed his waking hours and his dreams, too. He had been assuming that he would ride Paint, but Touch the Sky would not allow it.

"You will ride Brave One," he said.

"No!" Noisy Horse protested. "I want to ride Paint."

Touch the Sky spoke firmly. "First *you* have to learn how to hunt buffalo. It takes practice and courage to run alongside them. Brave One will teach you that. Only then can you teach Paint."

Noisy Horse ground his moccasin into the dust.

"Son, buffalo hunting is dangerous. Many things can go wrong. It is foolishness to put an inexperienced rider on an inexperienced horse."

Noisy Horse knew he must respect his father's wishes, but he felt angry, and he let it show.

🐎

On the first day of the hunt, people milled around, gathering possessions, singing, drumming, and dancing. Paint pranced with her head high. Noisy Horse sensed that she was as keen to go hunting as he was. He talked to her, repeating the words that Touch the Sky had told him.

"Hunting is dangerous, Paint. I don't want you to get hurt. Soon we'll hunt buffalo together. In the meantime you must wait here." Paint nosed his hand, hard. He should have reprimanded her, but he didn't have the heart.

That first hunt showed Noisy Horse the wisdom of his father's words. He was accustomed to seeing the buffalo grazing peacefully way off in the distance, or lying dead with their legs sticking straight out. Even lifeless, their great bulk was formidable, but galloping alongside the stampeding herd was more frightening than he had ever imagined. When a cow tossed her massive head at him, threatening to charge, his heart pounded and his limbs weakened. Her power was fearsome. Noisy Horse knew then that it was true: a buffalo could gore a horse and rider with its horns and fling them both into the air like soft dolls. And this cow was just one of hundreds.

Noisy Horse had carried a rifle that day, but he didn't use it. It took all of his skill to keep Brave One galloping next to the buffalo. He knew it would take more practice to learn how to release his grip on the reins, reach for his rifle, aim, and fire. He needed both physical and emotional skills. He needed to trust his horse. And he couldn't trust Paint yet. Not entirely. Not with his life. She startled too easily. Just recently a bird had flown up from the grass under

Paint's hooves. She had spun and bolted, taking Noisy Horse by surprise. He'd lost his balance, flying from her slippery back and landing painfully on his shoulder. Touch the Sky had said that a wild mustang on the plains needed to react quickly and gallop away from an unexpected predator. It was a trait that could save her life. But with a rider on her back it was not a good trait. And on a buffalo hunt it could be fatal for both horse and rider.

"Paint is still only three," Touch the Sky explained. "She is much like you, my son! Not yet an adult, although she thinks she is! And, like you, she will challenge authority. Sometimes you obey me and your mother, knowing that we are your parents, but other times it is hard for you to accept. It's the same with Paint. She respects you in many ways, and allows you to be her leader, just as she accepts Tika is her leader in the herd. But she will challenge you. Young ones always challenge the old ones! She is bigger and stronger than you are, so it is important that you win these battles, even the small ones. When she fully accepts that you are boss, then you will have her trust."

Armed with his father's advice, Noisy Horse watched for moments when Paint tried to undermine his authority. The first time came sooner than he had expected. Paint ignored his gentle request to move away from Swift. The boy reacted strongly, banging both legs hard against her sides. Paint bounded forward, but then spun back toward her mother. Noisy Horse was ready. He grabbed the inside rein tight and forced Paint into the spin as if it was his idea instead of hers, banging his outside leg against her side and forcing her on past her mother and back to full circle.

Paint looked perplexed. She stopped and chewed her lip. Noisy Horse asked her to move forward once more, but after a few steps she tried again to spin back to her mother. But this time Noisy Horse wouldn't let her stop. He drove her on in tight circles as if he was the boss mare.

Noisy Horse could tell when the fight left her.

He relaxed his legs around her chest and released his hold on her head. Paint stood stock still, breathing hard.

Touch the Sky was pleased. "You did well, my son. You won!"

Paint chewed her lip.

"See!" Touch the Sky said, pointing to Paint's mouth action. "She's going over it in her mind, coming to terms with it. Next time, she'll think twice about challenging you."

Touch the Sky was right. From that moment on, Paint was different. Noisy Horse felt the tension leave her. Her relaxation told him that she was relieved to hand over the stressful job of being a leader, of taking responsibility, of making decisions. She seemed to say that life is much easier as a follower. Noisy Horse was elated, but he felt the weight of his new responsibility. In exchange for Paint's submission he must assure her that she was safe under his watchful eyes.

Soon Paint was moving her feet sideways, or backward, spurting from a halt to a gallop and sliding back to a halt, all with just the slightest movement of warm legs that straddled her back, and gentle hands that guided her head. Noisy Horse asked for Paint's cooperation, and she gave it. Sometimes she seemed to know what he wanted even before the young man moved a muscle.

Paint and Noisy Horse were becoming one.

CHAPTER FIVE

The day that government agents rode into the village with orders for the band to report to the Indian agency, father and son were miles from home, galloping across the prairie astride Paint and Swift, shooting at bones they'd piled up as target practice. With every shot, the young man's aim improved, and with every bullet that whistled past her ears, Paint's fear diminished. Despite the commotion around her, she seemed to know that Noisy Horse would keep her from harm.

Touch the Sky was proud of both his son and the painted horse. Finally he agreed that the pair was experienced enough to hunt buffalo together.

Noisy Horse was ecstatic, and couldn't wait to tell everyone. But when they arrived home everyone was talking about far more important issues. Touch the Sky quickly agreed with the other elders. They would not comply with orders from the Big White Chief. They would not move to where the government wanted them to go, even though there was a promise of food. They would stay on their ancestral land, living the traditional life of hunting buffalo, moving only to find fresh grazing for the horses and to follow the migrating herds. It was settled.

For generations the buffalo had passed this way at this time of year. The People were in the right place, and it was the right time. But weeks passed and the buffalo did not come.

The women rationed the meat. Everyone had an edge to their hunger. The faces of the children were gaunter than they had been when the buffalo were plentiful, when great herds regularly migrated across the plains.

The People dismantled their dwellings, transforming the long poles and buffalo hides into drags to transport the old ones, the young ones, and all their possessions. Then they followed the drying river bed north and west, in search of buffalo.

From each new base camp, Noisy Horse and Touch the Sky rode out, for days at a time, their eyes scouring the horizon for the dark form of a distant herd.

But there was nothing.

The summer sun was hot and no rain fell. There was still prairie grass for the horses to eat, but it was dry and brown and lacked nutrition. The bloom started to fade from their glossy coats.

"Before the white men brought rifles," Touch the Sky told his son, as they rode side by side across the empty plain, "our ancestors killed buffalo with lances."

Noisy Horse couldn't imagine the courage, skill, and strength it took to hurl a lance into a buffalo.

"And before that, they hunted buffalo with bows and arrows!"

Noisy Horse was horrified at the idea of trying to kill a buffalo with something as flimsy as an arrow, like the one he used to pick off birds for the stew pot.

"That was a long, long time ago," Touch the Sky said, "before the white man brought horses to this land."

"The white men brought horses?" the boy queried, shocked that there was a time when the People did not have horses. As far as he was concerned horses were part of him, part of his identity, part of his culture. He could not imagine his People without horses. He could not imagine life without horses.

Touch the Sky sucked his teeth. "Horses were the only good thing they brought to our land."

"But why did the white man give us horses?" Noisy Horse asked, knowing that the white men were a people of takers, not givers. "What did we give them in return?"

Touch the Sky chuckled. "They never planned to give us horses. They brought horses here for their own purpose, and one of those purposes was to hunt us to extinction. But some of their horses escaped. They lived wild and free on the plains, and they flourished."

"So we tamed the wild horses?"

Touch the Sky grinned. "Yes, but we stole horses

from the white men, too. The white men stole many things from us so it seemed the right thing to do."

The summer was over by the time they finally spotted buffalo and the hunt began. Paint didn't need any urging. She broke into a gallop. Noisy Horse thought the mare was going flat out. It was as fast as he had ever ridden her. But they needed to catch up with the stampeding herd, so he thumped his legs against her sides and she responded with a fresh burst of speed that took his breath away. They soon caught up with a full-grown cow. Her tongue lolled from her mouth and she was beginning to tire. She tossed her head toward Paint and for a horrible second Noisy Horse thought she was going to charge; but she didn't, she kept running. He let go of Paint's reins, trusting that she would stay straight, and reached over his shoulder for his rifle. He aimed for the cow's chest behind the front legs and fired. It was a perfect shot, but she didn't fall. She ran on for a while, slowing, weakening. Paint slowed, too, no longer encouraged to race by her rider.

Time stood still for Noisy Horse. He looked into the dark eye of the buffalo, who was trying to take a few more steps, fighting with all her strength to hang on to life. The remaining buffalo thundered past, but Noisy Horse hardly saw them. He had eyes for nothing but this one creature whose life was ending, who was collapsing on the ground so close to him. Paint watched too, although her wide eyes were also looking out for danger. She sensed that Noisy Horse, at this very moment, was unable to be her leader. It made her nervous. She became more attuned to her surroundings, her ears swivelling, her eyes wide open and rimmed with white, her muscles trembling.

The cow was down. Blood oozed from the wound in her chest. Her tongue, studded with pieces of earth, hung from her gasping mouth. Blood and saliva frothed from her wet nostrils with each snort. Noisy Horse wished she would die. He wanted it to be over. He knew that by tradition he had just become a man. He didn't feel like a man.

Touch the Sky pulled up alongside. "Shoot her in the head, son, it will be quicker that way."

Noisy Horse looked aghast. His father nodded. "It's the right thing to do. I'll do it for you, if you can't."

Noisy Horse took aim and fired. The impact made the buffalo jump a little, but after that she was still.

Touch the Sky and the other hunters rode in circles around Noisy Horse and Paint, shouting their praises. But Noisy Horse felt hollow. He had taken the life of a mighty buffalo, and even if it meant that his family would eat, he didn't like the way killing made him feel.

CHAPTER SIX

The band spent the winter in the foothills, where rain fell as snow. They gave thanks to the Great Spirit, and to the buffalo who had given their lives so that they themselves might have meat for their bellies and thick hides for warmth. The horses browsed on the trees and pawed through the snow to find grass, and when the temperature dropped they huddled together. But with the first signs of spring, the people packed up their tipis once again and headed back to the grassland.

Paint was the first to feel the ground tremble. It began with a slight sensation in her teeth as she cropped the low grass, then she felt it in her hooves. She recognized it instantly, the drumming rhythm of many cantering horses. They were a long way off, but she could tell they were coming closer. She had no fear, just curiosity. She lifted her head and stood still, ears pricked, nostrils flared, listening, smelling, watching.

Noisy Horse was guarding the herd that day, making sure they didn't stray too far, watching for wolves that might try to steal one of the new foals. He saw Paint's head come up, and immediately his eyes followed her intent gaze. He knew she was seeing or hearing something, but she didn't appear anxious or fearful. In fact she seemed filled with expectation, so he knew she hadn't spotted wolves. It was likely a herd of mustangs. As much as the young man enjoyed watching the wild horses, he hoped that today it was not mustangs on the horizon. He hoped it was buffalo. The family needed to eat. They were all hungry. There had been no spring hunt. There had been no buffalo! Not since the previous autumn when he and Paint had made their first kill together. Touch the Sky said that the buffalo had gone to live far from the white men who swarmed across the plain like a plague of grasshoppers. Noisy Horse had not seen the grass-hopping white men.

Paint was still immobile, alert, watching something in the distance, something that Noisy Horse could not see. He glanced at the rest of the herd. Swift seemed unperturbed. Her head was down and her neck stretched out to the full extent of the rope that held her. She was nibbling the grass in a circle around the wooden peg that he had pounded into the earth. Paint was free, as she always was. She could have galloped off, but Noisy Horse knew she wouldn't go far, especially without her mother. The other horses, too, were preoccupied with grazing. Except for Tika, the herd's blue roan leader. She was

46

tied within the circle of tipis, and was fretting, but she had been fretting for hours, wanting nothing more than to charge back to the herd and start nipping them all into line.

Noisy Horse kept watching, so he could sound the alarm, alerting the band at the first sign of buffalo. His stomach was tight with apprehension; everyone would rush around catching their horses, getting their guns and ammunition ready. Was it excitement he felt in his gut? Or was it dread? He didn't know. Another horse noticed Paint's observant stance and raised its head, too. Then they all flung up their heads and faced the still invisible visitors.

Noisy Horse didn't understand what he was seeing when a flag crested the gentle rise. It wasn't buffalo; of that he was sure. He leaped to his feet, then wasted a valuable second, mesmerized by the brown hats that bounced into view on the ridge, seemingly hundreds of them, bunched close together, shimmering in a haze of heat and dust. Then he saw horses' heads. He couldn't yet hear the jangle of their bridles, or the pounding of their hooves, but Paint could. She'd also scented an odour that was familiar and yet unfamiliar at the same time. It was different from that of Noisy Horse and his people. It was unsettling. Paint held her ground, intrigued, as the cluster of horses crested the ridge and started to bear down on the camp. But Noisy Horse had already spun around and was running toward the tipis, yelling "Grasshoppers! Grasshoppers!" He couldn't remember the word for soldiers.

Instantly the People were in disarray, falling over one another in their scramble to gather small children and run. Paint knew that something was badly wrong, and she trembled, her muscles tense, poised to take flight. The first rifle cracks sent her galloping flat out, away from the camp. It wasn't just the noise of the exploding rifles that frightened her, for she was accustomed to gunfire. She'd learned to tolerate it during the hours of target practice, and when she had galloped alongside the stampeding buffalo. More than the explosions, it was the screams from the People that terrorized her.

After a short distance, her blind panic subsided, enabling her to see other horses on her flanks, galloping stride for stride. With a slight sideways toss of her head, she saw that Swift was not far behind, dragging both the rope and the wooden peg. But Tika, who had been tied within the circle of tipis, was not with them. She was still back there, her high-pitched neighs demanding that the herd return. The panicked horses slowed and circled, crowding together, moving with short, jerky strides and violent head tosses. Unable to stay still, but unsure of where to go, they were caught between their urge to escape to safety and their urge to obey their leader.

Tipis crashed down.

The People shouted. Screamed. Wailed. Fell down. Moaned.

The soldiers yelled. Guns smoked.

The boss mare squealed and staggered. Horses broke away from the group in all directions; then, finding themselves alone, regrouped tightly, drawing courage from one another.

Tika struggled to stay on her feet, but her legs gave out and she crashed onto her side, thrashing the air, her legs still galloping in her futile attempt to get away.

And then she lay still.

The herd veered away from their fallen leader, bolting in a tight group. Heads against rumps. Hooves throwing up clods of earth. Legs tangling Swift's rope.

They galloped wildly across the open prairie, panic pushing them onward. Swift fell, but was back on her feet in an instant, racing on with bloodstained knees. The horses had no thought about where they were going, instinct telling them only that they must get away from the danger, from the guns that made horses lie on the ground against their will, from the predators who would eat them. Swift was at the back of the group now, the rope flailing around her legs, occasionally making her stumble again. But she didn't fall. She braced her head and neck in anticipation and galloped on.

Paint was one of the fastest horses in the herd. She could have kept up with the leaders, but she stayed back with her mother, far enough away to avoid the trailing rope, but close enough to feel Swift's hot breath, close enough to be flecked with her saliva.

The herd tore down the dry riverbed like a flash flood, leaping over boulders worn smooth from an eternity of fast-flowing water. Some of the horses chose a different route around rocks that were too large to leap, but just like a fast moving river held tightly between its banks, they soon converged again and flowed on as one.

Back on higher land, they leaped off rocky outcrops and charged through sage brush, oblivious to their pounding hearts. Swift straggled behind, Paint with her.

Without warning, Swift somersaulted into the air, landing with an earth-shaking grunt. Paint planted her front feet and came to an abrupt halt in a single stride, dust rising around her in a cloud. She trotted back to her mother. Swift was flat on her side, not moving. Paint lowered her head and reached out to touch Swift's muzzle, nickering softly, begging her to get back to her feet, to continue their flight to safety. But Swift was motionless. The dust settled. Suddenly the old mare was scrambling with her forelegs, trying to heave herself up, but she screamed and collapsed to the ground. She tried repeatedly, struggling to breathe, becoming more and more frantic, knowing, as all grass-eaters do, that her life would soon be over unless she could get on her feet and run.

Paint nudged her mother, gently at first, then vigorously, pushing her nose under Swift's chest, trying to help her rise, just as Swift had once done for her when she was a helpless foal. Swift pawed and clawed with her front hooves, then, with a scream that filled Paint with terror, she dragged her hindquarters upright and stood panting through flared nostrils.

The other horses had disappeared over the horizon. They hadn't even slowed. Swift's heaving sides revealed the agony she was in. Paint nibbled her mother's sweat-drenched neck, then continued on down her spine in what she knew was Swift's favourite grooming routine. Swift squealed and flicked her tail into Paint's face. Paint retreated, mouthing, licking, chewing.

Swift stood for a long time, her eyes glazed, her lips pursed, her hindquarters slewed sideways so that the tip of one hoof barely touched the ground. Paint rested, too, head to rump with her mother, flicking her tail to keep the insects from Swift's face. Paint went through several cycles of resting alternate hind legs, but Swift didn't move. Except to swing her head, teeth bared, when Paint reached out to nudge her hindquarters.

By this time the herd had long gone. Paint sniffed the air, hoping to catch their scent, but the odour of something else filled her nostrils: fire! It was not the comforting smell of burning buffalo dung, or even the disturbing stench of cooking meat. This scent reeked of fear and destruction. Paint looked back. A dark ribbon snaked upward, then billowed out like a cloud and faded into the clear blue sky. She watched for a long time, until the smoke vanished and its scent disappeared from the wind, until the sun sank low on the horizon.

Paint was thirsty. She needed to find a stream,

but Swift made no attempt to walk. She stood on three legs, her head low, her breathing laboured. Paint grazed close to Swift, finding the wooden peg that earlier in the day had held Swift's rope so that she couldn't wander far from the tipis. It was firmly wedged between the rocks. Paint eyed it suspiciously, alert for danger, aware of a new sense of responsibility. In the past, Swift, or Tika, or Noisy Horse had always watched out for *her*, and even though she had often challenged their authority, Paint had been a follower, not a leader. Now everything had changed. She had to assume leadership. She wanted to lie down and rest after the long gallop and the stress. She didn't. She stood at her mother's side and watched over her.

Wolves came that night. They arrived on soft pads, stealing soundlessly through the short grass, but Paint knew they were there. She could smell them. Fear rushed through her. She nipped at her mother's flanks, telling her they must go. But Swift sighed and hung her head lower still. Paint cantered in circles around her, unable to remain motionless, every fibre in her body insisting that she run.

A pair of eyes gleamed in the weak moonlight, and for an instant terror immobilized Paint. But then she swung her quarters around and lashed out with both hind legs. The wolf loped away a few paces, then stood waiting, watching. Paint turned to face the predator, bearing down on him, stomping the earth, matching his snarl with her own bared teeth. He backed up, keeping just out of range. In a violent surge, she leaped toward him, striking out with her front hooves. His skull crumpled under her blow. He keeled over and was still.

Paint turned back to her mother, but it was too late. One wolf was already crouching on her back like a human rider in flight. Another had sunk his teeth into her rump, but Swift was not lashing out at him. There was no fight left in her. A third grabbed her muzzle. Swift tossed her head weakly, struggling for breath, but she lacked the strength to lift the predator from his feet. At that moment, Paint knew that her mother had given herself to the meat-eaters. Swift's acceptance of death flowed over Paint, too. Even if she had been able to fight off the wolf pack, instinct told her she should not intervene. She retreated a few steps. In her peripheral vision she saw other shadowy wolf forms, but she felt no threat from them. They were waiting for Swift to fall. They would not risk injury by attacking her when Swift was so close to death.

Swift's knees folded, as if she was settling her body to roll in the sand. She waited for a second, poised in a bow to her attackers, then her hindquarters smacked down. The wolves ripped into her belly immediately, fighting among one another with bared teeth and savage jaws. Swift moaned softly.

For Paint, the smell of spilled intestines gave rise to a fresh frenzy of fear. She bolted into the darkness.

CHAPTER SEVEN

Paint raced on throughout the night, constantly sniffing the air for traces of her own kind, hoping to ease her growing loneliness by joining a herd. When the sun came up, her eyes confirmed what her nostrils had already told her: she was the only horse on a never-ending plain.

Driven by unbearable thirst, she searched for water. Toward the end of the day she was knee-deep in a stream, drinking long and hard. The water was sweet. And close to the water's edge the grass was lush. Trees grew along the bank and offered shade from the hot sun. It was a perfect place for horses. She would wait for them to come.

But the only animals that approached were pronghorn antelope. They looked at her intently before timidly moving past to drink some distance downstream. Loneliness weighed on Paint so heavily that when they bounded back across the grassland she followed them, until their agitation told her they were scared of her. They didn't want her around.

Paint headed back to the stream and followed it across the open grassland. Along its edge, the grass had been worn away and the earth was hard-packed. It made the going easier, and before long she was half-asleep, head low, ears flopped sideways, legs moving automatically, hooves thudding quietly in the dust.

When her feet trod on a pile of stale horse droppings, she was instantly alert. The droppings were almost odourless, but when she blew moist breath into them, there was enough scent for her to know that they weren't from any horse she knew. But at least they were from a horse!

Paint put more energy into her step and trotted along briskly, all of her senses attuned to her surroundings. The stream was wider now and the trail along its bank well-trodden. There were more horse droppings scattered on the trail and then a mound of fresh ones. She nudged them with her nose, snorting and inhaling the aroma, trembling with excitement. Then she raised her head to look around.

Far into the distance Paint saw a horse. She whinnied as loudly as she could, her body vibrating with the effort. The other horse raised its head and neighed a friendly greeting in return. Paint was surprised, however, when a second horse also answered her call. She couldn't see it, but it was close, its sweat-laden scent wafting in the breeze. Another odour mingled with the exciting smell of warm horse; it was human. One scent told her to flee; the other told her to approach. Before she did either, a horse ambled around a bend in the trail. He nickered softly. Everything about the big palomino was friendly, except that he carried a strange-smelling man on his back.

Paint's longing to be with other horses kept her rooted. Suddenly something flew over her head and tightened around her neck. She pulled back, struggling at the end of the man's rope, but it was looped around the horn on the palomino's saddle, and she found herself pulling against *him*. He was bigger and stronger than she was, and he braced against her efforts. She didn't struggle for long. Her heart wasn't in it. She wanted to make friends with this horse and find her place in his herd.

"Well, look at what we got here. A painted horse!" the man said. "D'ya reckon she's a mustang?"

There was no other human around and no one talked back to the man.

"What d'you think, Cruiser? She's a good-looker for sure. She's standing there good and quiet now. I reckon she's had a bit of training. I'm guessing she ain't wild, not like a mustang that just walked in off the plain. If that were the case she'd still be swingin' around on the end of the rope."

With pricked ears and soft eyes, Cruiser stretched his head toward Paint and blew softly into her nostrils. There was no malice in his greeting. Paint blew back, delighting in the closeness of another horse. They nickered softly, getting to know each other, while the man continued talking to himself.

"Are you an Indian pony? Indians like the spots and the paints. If they trained you as one of their buffalo-hunting horses, you're gonna make my life one heck of a lot easier."

Suddenly Paint flattened her ears, squealed, and

gave Cruiser a warning strike with her foreleg. The gelding was confused. But the man understood. "Mares!" he exclaimed, turning the palomino back the way they had come. "She's gonna be top dog, Cruiser old boy. You're gonna have to watch your p's and q's."

Even if the rope was not around Paint's neck, she would have followed Cruiser down the trail, her instinct telling her that she was safer with this horse and man than alone. Before long they came to some buildings. They were unlike the tipis she was accustomed to. A wisp of dung-scented smoke rose from the top of one. It was a familiar smell and it soothed her anxiety. The man dismounted and looped Cruiser's reins over a hitching rail. Then he startled Paint by grabbing her head, forcing her mouth open to inspect her teeth.

"Never look a gift horse in the mouth," he said, laughing at his own joke. "You're still young! Six going on seven, I reckon. Today's my lucky day!"

The man disappeared inside the shack, reappearing with a halter, which he tried to put onto Paint. His movements were rapid and rough, making Paint toss her head and fidget. He wrestled with her, poking his elbow into her neck and pushing the headpiece forcefully over her ears by flattening them hard against her skull. Finally, when her ears popped back into position, he yanked the buckle tightly around her jaw. Then he tied her to a post, so tight she couldn't get her head down to the ground.

She didn't like the man, and felt no desire to be

with him, but Cruiser was friendly. He stood close, his tail swishing the flies from both their hindquarters. Soon his bottom lip flapped and his eyes glazed over. In his relaxed, sleepy presence, Paint felt calmer and safe. She could have gone to sleep, too, but the horse she had originally seen in the distance held her attention. He was pacing back and forth on the same path, his tail and head high and his ears pricked, telling Paint that he wanted to come and meet her, but something prevented him. She didn't know what. But it seemed to Paint that he was watching out for danger, so she rested a leg and napped alongside the palomino.

The big man's voice woke them up. He was carrying two buckets.

"Just a taste for you, my girl," he said, slackening the rope so Paint could get her head in the bucket. "You probably ain't used to oats and corn. Anyways, first I need to see if you're worth keeping, if you're worth the cost of good feed. So I plan on getting up on you, to see what you can do."

Paint was still licking the bottom of the bucket when something flapped onto her back, spreading its wings and settling like a bird. She hadn't seen it coming and was surprised. She yanked her head out of the bucket so fast she knocked the skin from her nose.

"It's just a saddle blanket. Ain't you ever had one of these before?"

The object had stopped flapping, and since there were still a few oats trapped in the corners of the pail, Paint got back to work with her tongue, trying to dislodge them. Warily she kept one eye on the man, who reappeared, dragging something else.

"Let's see how you are with this," he said, allowing her to briefly sniff the leather before tossing it onto her back and settling it on top of the blanket. Paint stood stock still as he rocked the heavy Western saddle back and forth into the right position.

"That's not so bad, is it? I'll just tighten it up with the cinch."

With that he reached under her belly for the dangling strap and quickly pulled it tight, securing everything to her back. Paint didn't like the feeling and kicked up with a hind leg, trying to dislodge it all. The man brought his knee up hard into her flank.

"You'll get used to it in a minute or two," he said, leading her around in circles. The saddle squeaked, sending her forward in a lunge. The man grabbed the rope firmly. She couldn't escape, so instead she danced on the spot. The saddle creaked and flapped even more.

"Whoa, there, it's just the fenders flapping against your sides. I'm guessing you haven't had one of these on your back before. Indians don't go in for saddles, do they? Bloody heathens! They just leap on and off and ride around bareback. Gotta respect them as horsemen, though."

As soon as Paint could walk around without the saddle scaring her, the man brought her back to Cruiser's side. He disappeared into the shack and reappeared with something else.

"Ever had a bit in your mouth?" he asked, sticking his fingers into the corners of her mouth, prying it open and forcing in a metal rod. He was so quick that before Paint knew what was happening, he'd pulled the straps over her ears and tightened everything up, clamping the bit on top of her tongue. She tried to spit it out, but to no avail. She moved her jaw in all directions, but the bit clonked painfully against her teeth.

"The bit's too low," he said. "I need to bring it up a notch." He adjusted the buckles on both sides until the bit crinkled the corners of her lips. She chomped and chewed for a while as he looked on. "You'll get used to it," he said, retying her to the post and walking off.

Her mouth eventually got weary of trying to move the bit out of the way and she turned her attention to the buckskin horse that was still pacing up and down in the same place. Paint stared intently. The sun glinted on something. The buckskin was not free on the prairie as she had thought. He was contained behind strands of something that looked as fragile as cobweb.

The man reappeared. "Okay, horse, I'm trusting that the Indians taught you a thing or two, so I'm gonna get up on you now. I'm too old to ride broncs. I've done too much of that in my life. So you'd better behave."

He put his foot in the stirrup and dragged himself into the saddle. Paint stood still, until the metal wheels on the man's heels dug into her sides. She leaped forward. He yanked on the rein. The bit dug into her mouth. She flung her head high.

"Easy there, easy," he said, but his voice did little to reassure her. She tried her best to evade the pain by doing what he asked of her. As a result, they moved forward in fits and starts.

"I reckon I can take the spurs off my boots," he said. "You don't need 'em like the others. I'm Abraham, by the way. You can call me Abe." He laughed uproariously. "Gets to be something when you introduce yourself to a horse!"

Over the next few days, Abe and Paint experimented together, walking, loping, galloping, stopping, reining back, circling. Paint did it all. When Abe was heavy-handed, she tossed her head, chomped the bit, and salivated so much that flecks flew back and splattered Abe's leather chaps. He soon learned to lighten his hands. And when he was heavy-legged she shot forward, leaving him lagging behind in the saddle. He didn't like that much, so he learned to ask with kinder legs, nudging rather than kicking. And he didn't like it when she trotted. He wanted her to miss that gait and go from a walk straight to a lope. That worked for Paint, too, because when Abe banged around on her back at a trot it was uncomfortable for her as well as for him.

"Well, you're gonna be my new riding horse," he announced. "Cruiser's getting up there in age. The clients can ride him. He's safe as houses for those city-slickers. They've got no horse sense. I reckon you'd toss 'em off in no time!"

CHAPTER EIGHT

Most of the clients who came to Abe's Buffalo Hunting Company were brash, or ignorant, or brutal men. But they all had one thing in common: they wanted to be buffalo hunters, albeit for a day or two.

They came from the big cities, craving "the real wild west experience" that Abe promised, yet they had little horse sense. They always asked to ride the striking black-and-white painted horse — the Indian horse! But Abe had learned that Paint was sensitive and didn't do well with ham-fisted beginners.

On this day, as always, Paint and Abe led the trek to find the buffalo. Cruiser followed, carrying the client from the city, and the buckskin, pulling the rattling cart, brought up the rear. On days when there were several clients, they would ride in the wagon, holding the reins, believing they were steering Buck. But the buckskin knew what he was doing without a driver. He was content to follow the other two horses.

A prairie dog nosed out of his hole. Paint didn't jump sideways as she might have when she was young and inexperienced, but her muscles tensed all the same. Even Abe felt it. When he had first started riding the painted mare, he would not have picked up on this small indication of Paint's anxiety, but over time Abe had learned to read her body language. He had come to realize that when he was loud and forceful, she was tense and flighty. So in her own way Paint taught Abe to adjust his riding style to a slightly gentler one. Abe reckoned that he and Paint had become the perfect team. He didn't know that their relationship fell far short of the almost psychic connection that Paint had once had with the young man called Noisy Horse.

"It's just a gopher!" Abe said, sucking his teeth. "We're looking for buffalo, remember."

At the sound of the human voice, the gopher twirled and scurried back down his hole in a puff of dry soil. Abe nudged Paint forward with his heels. She responded with more energy in her step, Cruiser once more tucking in behind her, and the buckskin behind him. It was the order that all three horses favoured.

The scent of buffalo teased Paint's nostrils. She raised her head, inhaling the trace of scent on the wind. Abe paid attention, too.

"What's up, girl? Can you smell 'em?"

The mare walked slowly, her delicate black ears pricked forward, her eyes focused, straining to hear or see the big grass-eaters. But she saw nothing. And apart from the conversation between Abe and the city-slicker, she heard only the groaning of the wagon wheels, the footfalls of horses, and the buzz of insects bursting up from under their hooves. This was a quiet place; no trees to creak, no leaves to quiver, no streams to gurgle. Just prairie grass, wild-flowers, and a few tall grasses rustling in the breeze.

Paint had been leading the procession for a while, and as such, she had been constantly alert, watching out for danger ahead. It was tiring, and she needed to rest. As soon as Abe slumped in the saddle, Paint took advantage of his daydreaming. She slowed her pace, and by letting her ears flop sideways, she gave Cruiser permission to pass. The palomino pricked his ears, chomped his bit, and took the lead. Paint ducked in behind him. Then she lowered her head and ambled along, half-asleep, secure in the knowl-edge that Cruiser was watching for danger ahead, and that Buck, straining against the traces of the rumbling cart, was watching for a sneak attack from the rear. The three horses had been together long enough to trust each other with their lives.

A jerk on the reins brought Paint back to wake-fulness. Instinctively she tossed her head into the air, pushed her nose to the sky, and skidded to a halt. Abe usually relaxed his grip on the reins when she did this, but he was distracted and kept a tight hold on her mouth. She bent her head to her chest, try-ing to escape the pain of the bit. But Abe still held on with clenched fists. She moved backward a few steps, certain that this was what he wanted her to do, but he dug his heels into her sides, making her leap forward. She got another jab in the mouth, broke out in fresh sweat, and quivered. Abe usually yelled at times like these, but instead, his voice was hushed. "Settle down. You'll spook the buffalo."

Abe continued whispering, but this time to the man who rode Cruiser. "We're downwind of them, so they don't know we're here. But we need to find cover. See that ridge there? It's perfect. We'll leave the horses here, and go on by foot."

Abe swung one leg over Paint's rump. She braced in anticipation. He put all his weight in one stirrup and slowly eased himself to the ground, dragging the saddle sideways and moaning that he had stiffened up like a board. He rocked the saddle back into place, pulling some of Paint's hair in the process. The discomfort made her feel dispirited. She wanted to flex and bend her stiff back, but the ill-fitting saddle held her like a board.

Abe hooked the reins around the horn and grumbled. "That should stop you from stepping on 'em and breaking 'em again."

Paint sensed Abe's irritation, and she tensed her jaw, expecting a jab in the mouth that often accompanied this tone of voice.

Paint's back was hot and itchy, hairs were pulled the wrong way, and she had a sore spot where the hard leather had rubbed her. She wanted to get rid of the saddle from her back. She wanted to roll. She rubbed her head against Abe, but he didn't understand her discomfort. He didn't take the saddle off, or even loosen the cinch.

"You can graze for a spell," he said, slapping her

neck. She veered away from him, glad to be free, but he had hobbled her front legs and she stumbled. All she could do was mince away. Cruiser was hobbled too, and he followed Paint, shifting his weight back onto his hindquarters, then advancing his front feet in a half-rearing hop.

"Where are the hobbles for this one?" the city-slicker whispered, pointing to Buck, who was still attached to the cart.

"He don't need hobbles. So long as Paint and Cruiser are here, he won't go nowhere."

Abe and the city-slicker bellied to the edge of the rocky outcrop. It was not high, just a few feet above the level of the grassland. In fact, if Paint raised her head, she could look past the ridge and watch the buffalo grazing the sedges and prairie grass. The herd didn't know the men were close. The wind was blowing toward the horses. It carried the grass scent of the buffalo to Paint, along with the meat scent of the humans, and the quiet man-voices.

"There's no rush," Abe whispered, testing the rocks to find a secure support for his rifle. "See if you can spot the leader. She's the one we want first."

Paint didn't understand their words. She raised her head and peered over the ridge, watching the buffalo while trying to dislodge the wad of grass that had already clogged her bit. Accustomed to finding the leader in a herd of horses, she quickly discerned the buffalo boss. It was obvious in the way she tossed her head toward the calf who got irritatingly close. It was in the way another animal moved away from her when she lumbered up behind. The boss buffalo didn't need to use her immense power, or her great curved horns to have her way. No doubt, there had been times in the past when she had had to assert her dominance, but once her authority had been established she was able to lead without bullying.

This was obvious to Paint, but all plains buffalo looked alike to the city-slicker, who remained belly down on the ridge. He could tell only that the males were taller and heavier than the females, and the calves were smaller and lighter in colour than their mothers.

Paint worked her tongue back and forth and sideways, but the grass was tightly wrapped around the bit, caught in the jointed bar. Since there was little else to occupy her, she continued watching the herd. The buffalo boss knew Paint was there. She had seen the horse peering over the ridge, but she had no fear of other grass-eaters. She didn't put the herd on alert. The young ones still chased one another around like colts. The adults grazed, or chewed their cud lethargically.

They looked meek, but Paint knew better. She had run alongside them, had felt the ground tremble under their stampeding hooves. She had quaked at their power and aggression; like that of ten stallions in one raging beast. But she also knew they were less attentive to detail than horses. They didn't spook if a butterfly winged past their ear. They didn't watch for predators in the same way as horses. They were so big and powerful that an entire wolf pack would think twice before attacking a full-grown, healthy animal. The wolves would take only the old, the sick, the weak, or the young.

"One shot a minute," Abe advised, his voice so soft that Paint could barely hear him. "More than that and they panic. We want to keep 'em together as long as possible. Once they run, it's all over, for me at least, 'cause I ain't riding all over God's countryside chasing 'em. Make sure your rifle is well supported so you don't have to heft the weight of it, or you'll get mighty tired after a while."

The city-slicker did as he was told, settling into the cool grass.

"Have you found the leader yet?" Abe asked, after a few moments.

The city man shook his head. "If they were on the move the leader would be out front, I guess, but when they're bunched up like this grazing, how can you tell?"

"Look for an older cow," Abe whispered. "She'll pay more attention to her surroundings than the others. She'll raise her head occasionally and look around. See, there she is, the one with her head up, sniffing the air. I'll take her to show you how it's done. You can have the next. But don't shoot until I tell you. We mustn't spook 'em, remember. And don't bother with the young ones. Their hides ain't worth the effort of skinning. Don't waste your bullets on 'em. Go for the full-grown cows. Their robes fetch three or even four dollars apiece."

Abe wriggled forward, sighting his target. "Try

and get 'em sideways on, and aim for the chest, just behind the front legs. That way the bullet goes right into the lungs. It's an easy shot. Hell, you can hit her anywhere in the chest and you'll make a kill."

The sound of the rifle shot reverberated around the landscape, startling Paint. The first shot always had this effect on her. She lunged forward, instinctively trying to flee from the danger, but her forelegs were hobbled, and she staggered, losing her balance and falling to her knees. Her nose rested on the ground, steadying her while she used the power in her hindquarters to get back on all fours. Buck was running in circles around her, the cart rumbling after him.

The buffalo were startled, too, but they didn't run. They stared at the puff of white smoke drifting from the hidden rifle on the rocky ridge, but they saw no danger there. They looked to their leader, expecting her to run. They were poised to take flight after her. But although she jerked forward with the shot, she stopped dead and stood her ground. The others moved closer, sniffing the air, sensing no threat, other than the blood streaming from their leader's nostrils.

The boss buffalo struggled for a second to maintain her footing, but her legs gave way, and with a sudden lurch she crashed onto her side. Paint felt the earth shake right up through her hooves and into her gut. And she smelled blood. She wanted to bolt, but she couldn't. The hobbles restrained her.

The herd closed in around their fallen leader,

touching her with their wet, quivering noses, some of them bawling like cattle in distress. Paint could hear their confusion and their grief.

"Get ready," Abe whispered. "As soon as another animal starts to lead the herd away, you fire. The target's large. The range is close. The rifle's powerful with accurate sights. You can't miss."

This time the rifle shot only made Paint wince. The cow went down. Paint watched her hooves pawing the air futilely. She thrashed her massive head, blowing streams of red foam from her nostrils. Then she was still. Soon she was surrounded by others who touched her and started to bellow.

The two men took turns firing, bringing down the cows one by one. The herd clustered around the fallen, wide-eyed, unable to sense where the danger was coming from, unable to leave the dying. After a while Paint put her head down and grazed, barely flinching every time the rifle sent another bullet into the chest of yet another buffalo.

It may have appeared that Paint was no longer startled by the gunfire, no longer distressed by the smell of blood, or the presence of death. But unable to escape the horror around her, she had developed other ways of coping. She ground her teeth and chewed on fence posts. Abe complained about these things, putting it down to her bad habits. And when liquid manure rolled down her hind legs, staining the white markings, he grumbled because she made a mess of herself.

CHAPTER NINE

Once the shooting stopped, Paint looked out across the plain. All of the cows were on the ground. A few bulls were still standing, as well as most of the young ones.

"This isn't sport," the city-slicker said. "It's too easy."

"You're right. It's not sport. It's business. In less than an hour you and I have killed some fifty buffalo cows. The very best quality robes are on those animals. They're worth a lot of money. But if it's sport you want, follow me."

Abe grabbed his rifle and scrambled off the ridge. When he was out of sight of the herd, he strode toward Paint and grabbed the reins. He removed her hobbles and put them on Buck. "Sorry, old boy, but you have to stay put."

Abe heaved himself into the saddle, waited while the other man got on Cruiser, then he dug his heels into Paint's sides. "Let's have a bit of fun."

Paint broke into a canter and charged over the ridge. For the first time, the surviving buffalo saw their enemy. The bulls took fright and led the escape, the youngsters galloping after them. Abe held Paint's head in a tight rein, steering her alongside the fleeing animals. Then he set his sights on a bull. The explosion in Paint's ears gave her a fresh burst of speed. Cruiser thundered along behind, trying to keep up. The rifle shots goaded both horses to faster speeds until they seemed to be flying. Paint had done this before. She was good at it.

She galloped so close to a bull that his slobber smacked her on the neck.

Abe fired again and the bullet found its mark. The bull slowed. Within a few strides he staggered to the ground.

Behind them, the city-slicker downed a calf.

The others got away.

As soon as Paint and Cruiser returned from the chase, Buck stopped his constant neighing and hopped toward them as fast as his hobbles and his cart would allow. Paint pinned her ears, reminding him that he was at the bottom of the little herd of three. Then she greeted him warmly.

The men set to work skinning the buffalo. They pegged the skins on the short prairie grass, stretching them to the fullest extent while still warm and supple. A calf returned and stood by the corpse of its mother, bawling.

"I can't stand that racket," Abe complained,

grabbing a revolver from his hip and silencing the animal with a bullet.

The men kept working until the sun had almost disappeared. Then they lit a fire of dried buffalo dung. The city-slicker complained about the stink, but Abe said it would keep the wolves away.

Paint knew that wolves would come soon, lured from miles around by the scent of blood. It made her nervous.

Finally, Abe unhitched Buck from the cart and unsaddled Paint and Cruiser, tying all three to the cart. Then he speared slabs of buffalo meat and propped them over the fire to cook. Paint had become accustomed to the smell of death. It drifted from the kill sites, and lingered on the clothes of the humans. But these chunks of animal flesh so close to her nose brought a renewed sense of vulnerability. She snorted with anxiety.

"We've got enough buffalo steaks to feed all the folks in Washington," the city slicker said. "Seems a shame to let it rot."

Abe shrugged. "Ain't nothing we can do about it. We're here for the robes. That's all. We'll finish skinning tomorrow. By the time the stench of rotting meat attracts the wolves and the vultures, we'll have all the robes piled on the cart and be far away."

They ate their blackened meat and stretched out on the ground, their bellies stuffed. Instinct told Paint that now, just like stuffed wolves, the humans would not kill again for a while. She felt safer. She tried to roll to scratch her sore back and ease her aching muscles, but she was tied up. All she could do was tip her hindquarters to relax the muscles in one hind leg at a time. Her head lolled, her bottom lip drooped, her ears flopped, and her eyes glazed over.

The odour of wolf wafted into her sleep. Instantly she was on the alert. Buck and Cruiser were awake, too, and all three stood poised for flight. In a panic they tugged at their ropes. The cart groaned, but the brake was on and the wheels were chucked with blocks of wood, so it held fast. The horses snorted and shook their heads, hearts thumping, muscles quivering. But the wolves didn't come close. They skirted the camp, their pads soundless on the ground, eyes glinting in the moonlight.

"Something spooked the horses," Abe said, propping up his body on one elbow.

The city-slicker jerked upright. "What?"

"Wolves, probably."

The city-slicker grabbed his gun and scrambled to his feet.

"Don't worry," Abe said calmly. "They're not interested in us. They're not even interested in the horses tonight!"

"Wolves kill horses?" the city-slicker asked.

Abe was always surprised by the ignorance of his clients. "Sure! But they won't tonight, not when there's a banquet laid out for them on the prairie! They won't risk an argument with a horse. A single kick could break a shoulder, or a pelvis, or maybe smash a skull. I'm going to take a look, though. We don't want wolves spoiling our robes."

The first gunshot was so unexpected that the horses reared up, pawing the air, nostrils flaring. They jerked against their ropes, Paint pulling in one direction, Buck and Cruiser in another. But they soon settled, and silence returned quickly to the prairie.

However, for the rest of the night it seemed that every time Paint's head nodded toward the ground, a crack from the rifle startled her to wakefulness.

Finally, the sun rose over the horizon and the wolves vanished with the night.

Paint wrinkled her nostrils at the aroma of fresh coffee that mingled with the odour of entrails.

"Damn wolves ripped open one of the cows," Abe said.

CHAPTER TEN

The buffalo herds were becoming harder to find. Sometimes the hunters rode all day without finding a single animal to kill. That created a problem for Abe; the clients asked for their money back. He mulled over these things with Paint.

"It used to be so easy, but finding buffalo now is like looking for a needle in a haystack. And I'm too old to go traipsing all over the country. I've made a nice nest egg from selling robes. I'm thinking I should move east. I could have an easy life, have some luxury for once. Cattle are taking over the prairie now. Longhorns and shorthorns. That's where the money's at. Folks say I should start over as a cattle rancher. I have the horses. I have the skill. I have the land. I even have the cash to buy the cows. But I don't have the heart. I'll leave ranching for the young 'uns. I'll sell up and head east. But you, Paint, you'd make a good ranch horse. You could round up those cattle in a flash! It's second nature to you."

For most of the day, Buck, Cruiser, and Paint stood together in a small pen at the auction grounds, watching people parade by. Horses from other pens were led past them to a ring where everyone seemed to be yelling. As the day wore on, people started to leave, taking horses with them. When a man with a lead rope took Cruiser to the ring, Paint and Buck raised their heads as high as they could, but they could no longer see him.

A loud voice boomed. "Fifteen-year-old palomino! He's done a bit of everything. He'll round up your cattle and work the farm."

Another voice interrupted. "Fifteen! He's twenty if he's a day. Probably twenty-five! Look at those teeth. They're so long they're fit to fall out!"

"He's too old!" a voice yelled out. "He's good for nothin' but glue."

"Nonsense," the first voice answered. "There's years of work left in him. I'm willing to bet he's not a day older than sixteen."

Laughter rippled through the crowd.

"So what am I bid?" the booming voice asked.

There was no response.

Buck was next to be taken from the pen. Paint tried to charge through the gate, too, but it slammed in her face. She pawed the ground, then paced, then neighed, then stood with ears pricked, waiting for a reply. Buck answered. He was frightened, too.

"This buckskin is the best homesteader horse being sold today. He's big enough to pull your wagon out west, or north, or whichever way you're going. And strong enough to pull your plow when you get there. I hear it's a hard job turning over that buffalo grassland. The roots go down one heck of a long way. But this horse will make short work of it. He's only ten years old, so there's a lot of work left in him."

All of the voices were excited. They argued back and forth for a while. Paint was listening so attentively that she was surprised when someone grabbed her halter and led her out of the pen. She went willingly, keen to be reunited with Cruiser and Buck, but when she entered the ring they were nowhere in sight. Loneliness enveloped her and she neighed, her sides heaving with the effort. From a long way off, Cruiser answered. Buck answered, too. He was still close, and that comforted her, so she followed the man with the lead rope and walked with him in a circle.

"And now this magnificent painted horse."

The people on the edge of the ring started to walk away.

"I don't want no Indian horse. It probably ain't even broke."

"No sense paying good money for a mustang when I can go out and rope one for free!"

Paint recognized panic in the booming voice. "Sure, this horse looks like a mustang. And maybe she was trained by Indians. But she's been owned for the last few years by Abe Wilson at the Buffalo Hunting Company. Abe says you won't find a better horse in the land. He's only parting with her because he's heading back East. Abe's shot close to five thousand buffalo using this horse. She's accustomed to the sound of gunshots. She knows how to gallop hard and fast. And she's brave. Those buffalo weigh two or three times what this little horse does!"

"There ain't no call for a buffalo-hunting horse these days," someone said. "The buffalo have all gone! Just cattle now."

"Hey, Jeb, you should buy her as a cow pony. She'd probably take to that like a fish to water!"

"You might be right. And I came here today for a topnotch cow pony, but an Indian horse? I don't know. I want a solid bay or a black."

"You could sell her to Buffalo Bill Cody! I hear he's putting together a Wild West show with cowboys and Indians."

People laughed.

Despite Jeb's preference for horses of a solid colour, there was something about the painted mare that appealed to him. He liked the look in her eye. He decided to take a chance.

He bought Paint, tied her to the back of his wagon, and they headed northwest. Two days later they reached Longhorn Ranch in Eastern North Dakota.

CHAPTER ELEVEN

The year before buying the painted mustang, Jeb had made a homesteader claim on federal land. He was glad that he did, because all he had to do now was raise stock on the acreage and live on it for five years, and the title would be his!

North Dakota seemed to be the perfect place for cattle ranching. He wouldn't have to plant grass — it was already there! Rainfall was low, but the Great Plains had supported millions, if not billions, of wandering buffalo. Logic told him that there would be more than enough grass for a few hundred head of cattle and a handful of horses. Winters were cold, but cattle were hardy. They could fend for themselves unless there was a particularly cold snap, in which case they might need some hay to see them through. But the land had plenty of grass, and there was more than enough sun to turn it into hay. What's more, his cattle need not be confined to his own acreage. They could run on the range, a larger area of public land. At roundup time, ranchers would sort them and brand the new calves.

Jeb didn't know that rainfall on the Great Plains was unpredictable, and that every now and again the rain simply stopped falling, sometimes for months, sometimes for an entire summer, sometimes for years. The grassland became almost a desert then, and the buffalo moved on, searching a vast area for greener grass and water, migrating to the edges of the plain and into the foothills of the mountains. Also, Jeb didn't know that occasionally North Dakota had a winter that was a killer.

None of the ranchers knew these things because no white man had set foot on the plains until recently. All Jeb knew was that this vast expanse of natural grassland had been completely unproductive until he claimed it from the government. Now he had a stake in making it productive. There was a beef bonanza back east. It was easy money. He was going to be rich.

Paint had never seen cattle. To her, they were similar to buffalo in that they were grass-eaters and they moved in a herd. They were smaller than buffalo by far, and didn't have the massive heads and shoulders. Despite their long, curling horns, Paint sensed that the cattle were not as dangerous or as threatening as buffalo. They seemed docile in comparison.

Paint's first job on the ranch was to carry Jeb to check the fencelines. It was an easy task. They walked along the line for a while, then Jeb would dismount, take his tools from the saddle bags, tighten a strand of wire or replace a broken one. Then he got back on and rode a bit further. Jeb used a rawhide bosal on Paint, so there was no metal in her mouth. She soon realized that she didn't have to clench her teeth to protect herself from pain, as she had with Abe's long-shanked bit. And she was able to graze without battling the metal rod in her mouth. Not only did her jaw relax, but her whole demeanour softened.

After this introduction to ranch life, Jeb put Paint through her paces and came to the conclusion that she had natural talent at rounding up cattle. With a small amount of training she would be a great roping horse. Her lessons started right away. The bursts of speed and the sudden stops were natural movements for her, and Jeb was a good enough rider to make the most of her abilities.

Soon she was accustomed to the lasso flying past her ears, and had learned to brace backward, taking up the slack of the rope after the loop flew over a calf's head. Sometimes she had to stand alone while Jeb wrestled the calf to the ground. This was the hardest thing for her to learn.

It was a perfect summer with plenty of good grazing. Paint's ribs were well covered and she had a spring in her step. By midsummer the sun had bleached the shiny black patches in her coat, giving her gleaming red highlights. And her mane had red strands, too. The cattle were also healthy. They grew fast, gaining weight quicker than Jeb had even hoped for.

At the end of autumn, as the temperature started to drop, Paint's coat thickened and took on the texture of velvet. And one word was on everyone's lips: roundup. Paint could sense their anticipation.

The next morning, almost before the sun rose, every horse on the ranch was saddled and ready to go. The experienced ranch horses were eager, like the buffalo-runners had always been. It was contagious. Paint refused to stand still for Jeb to mount. She wheeled around him while he scrambled aboard. Other horses were almost galloping on the spot, keen to be through the gate and onto the range. Jeb sat astride Paint, yelling his orders to the riders, and then they were off.

After the first burst of speed, the horses settled into a slow lope. When cattle came into view, the riders guided their horses in different directions, skirting the animals and bringing them together in a closely knit group. The first time Jeb asked Paint to gallop after stragglers, he could sense her excitement. She bunched up, ready to buck, but Jeb felt it coming and kept her head up. He knew it was not a malicious buck. She was not trying to throw him from the saddle. She was bucking for joy, at the thrill of the chase! Jeb was excited, too. He let out a yahoo and waved his hat in the air.

When all of the stragglers were accounted for, the riders turned toward home, driving the cattle sedately in front of them, outriders keeping them in a group. Jeb rode in a quiet, relaxed manner and Paint matched his mood. She knew instinctively that rapid movements spooked cattle, just as they did horses, and picking up on Jeb's body language, she moved quietly. They sauntered peacefully toward home, the weary ranch hands speaking low and occasionally flapping their hats at a cow that looked ready to make a break for it. When the corral came into sight, Jeb tensed a little in the saddle and yelled a few instructions to other riders. "Keep them coming easy! Close up the right flank. That's it. Nearly there. Watch that one!"

A cow made a break on the far side. "Chuck! Wake up!" Jeb yelled. Paint whirled away toward the stray cow before Chuck came to his senses, and before Jeb even asked her to. With a swish of her tail, she galloped flat out and in seconds had skirted the herd, chased down the wayward cow, and driven it back to the others.

When the last cow was in the corral and the rails secured, the whooping and hollering started. Paint was startled by the hats that flew into the air and came back down like vultures. She ran backward in alarm, but the experienced ranch horses just swivelled their ears and kept their eyes on the moving targets. The cowboys were slapping each other on the back and making so much noise that Jeb had to yell to make himself heard.

"You've all worked hard today, and I thank you for that. But your horses have worked harder, so before you start on the whiskey, get the saddles off and turn the horses out. Don't start cooking your own grub until you've tended your horses. Chuck, fill up the water trough, and when you open up that pipe, count your blessings. Last week you were dragging the water up in buckets, and now the windmill does the job for you!"

As soon as Jeb turned Paint out into the pasture, she strolled to the sandy area where dust bowls had been created by countless rolling animals. Jeb draped his arms over the railing and watched the horses. It was one of his favourite ways to pass the time. A grey gelding was pawing the ground, looking for the perfect spot to roll. Paint approached purposefully, her ears pinned. The horse trotted away and Paint took over the vacated spot.

Jeb couldn't help but laugh. "Will you look at that," he mused aloud. "She's moving her way up the pecking order."

Paint sniffed the ground and pawed vigorously, kicking dirt into the air. Then she bent her knees neatly under her, lowered her chest gently to the ground, and let her hindquarters flop wearily down. Groaning, she stretched her head and neck along the sand, rubbing the sweat from her skin and scratching her face where the bridle had rubbed. Then she kicked her legs, heaved her body onto her back, and wriggled the sand into the sore spots on her spine. She didn't roll to the opposite side, however. She stood up and shook violently, sending a cloud of dust into the air, then repeated the routine on the other side. Covered in dirt, she jumped to her feet, grunted, and bolted off to where the other horses were grazing. She charged toward them with neck outstretched and ears clamped to her head. They tucked their tails and scooted away. Paint slid to a stop and began to nibble the grass where they had been.

"She'll be the boss in no time!" Jeb mumbled, walking off to join the men back at the corral.

Smoke was rising from a campfire and soon someone was strumming a guitar; others were singing.

"Gawd, you all sound like a pack of wolves," someone joked.

Half a mile away, Paint lifted her head and pricked her ears to the distant strains. Briefly she thought the same thing.

CHAPTER TWELVE

Just before sunrise, Jeb rang an old school bell. This made the ranch hands grouchy. They complained of headaches and not getting enough sleep, but after some coffee, they set to work with hammers, nails, wire, and rails, making chutes and gates and pens. With everything in place, the herd was driven down a narrow chute just wide enough for one cow at a time.

A cowboy sat on the railing at the end of the chute, manning a gate that sent each animal into one of three pens. The calves born that spring were sent into one pen. The steer from the previous spring were sent into another. And the heifers were returned to the range along with the breeding cows and a few bulls. Jeb was still building up his herd, so he planned to keep the young females another year. By then they would have calves of their own.

After the animals were divided up, Paint's job was to help rope the calves. The animals were fast, and not used to being handled, but they didn't seem to mind Paint walking close to them. Jeb was able to lean out from the saddle and loop the lasso over their heads. That scared them and they tried to yank away. Paint had to brace herself while Jeb jumped down to hog-tie them. One by one, each animal was immobilized, crying pitifully as the red hot branding iron was jammed against its rump. Paint's nostrils twitched at the smell of singeing hair and burning flesh. By the time the ropes were untied and the indignant calf scrambled to its feet and charged away, Jeb and Paint had caught another for branding and castrating.

It took the entire day to finish the job, but just before nightfall all of the calves were released to join the bulls and breeding cows on the range. Only the steer remained in the pens.

Early the next morning the horses were saddled again to start the cattle drive to the railway station, a journey of a good five miles down the rutted road. The steer were troublesome at first, frequently trying to break away. The horses and riders were hard-pressed to keep them together, but eventually apathy set in and the animals seemed content to amble along.

Paint had seen trains before, but only in the distance, puffing across the landscape. She had never been this close to one. She took a good look at it, and was ready to spook, but Jeb wasn't the slightest bit anxious, and that calmed her. Fortunately the train on which the cows were making their final journey was stationary and the engines were not as yet stoked. The cattle car was open with a wooden ramp in place. Cowboys and horses blocked escape routes, giving the animals just one choice: the cattle car. The leading steer walked up the ramp and the others followed.

"The first round's on me," Jeb announced, as soon as the door of the cattle car slammed shut. The cowboys were happy about that, joking and laughing as they rode around the corner to the saloon on Main Street. They hitched their horses to the rail outside the bar, and went in. All of the horses knew the routine, except for Paint. With heads hung low they went to sleep. Paint nodded off, too.

The sudden hiss of steam from the train jerked her awake. She reacted instinctively, yanking her head back, snapping the reins and bolting down Main Street, desperate to outrun the snorting creature that chugged along behind her. The other horses were still hitched to the rail and they turned to watch Paint disappear into the distance. None of them seemed unduly perturbed, either by Paint's escape or by the moving train. They switched their weight to different legs and dozed off again.

The piercing whistle urged Paint on, but the train was gathering speed, gaining on her, its one bright eye shining like the sun and its massive head shovelling the ground like a giant buffalo clearing snow. With great snorts of angry breath it drew alongside her. Suddenly there were no more buildings penning her in. Paint veered off into the open grassland, fleeing for her life.

Belching steam and with a scream from its

whistle, the train went straight on. A few seconds later Paint realized that the monster was no longer chasing her. Heaving from exertion, she slowed to a walk, her head held high, still searching for danger. There was none, but she didn't feel safe. The fear wouldn't leave her. She was on her own and she didn't like that. In the distance she heard the creature scream one more time. It sounded like an eagle. Anxiously, she snatched a mouthful of grass and chewed rapidly, her eyes wide. And then, just as if nothing had happened, she ambled back to where she remembered the horses were tied. They were still there, still hitched to the rail, still sleeping. She sidled in and did the same.

A little later, when all the men piled out of the bar, Jeb found Paint standing where he had left her. The only difference was that her reins were broken. He scratched his head, unable to figure it out, then knotted the broken ends together and rode back to the ranch.

CHAPTER THIRTEEN

From the moment Jeb claimed the government land, he'd started working on a long-range plan. At each annual roundup, he'd held onto most of his heifers to build up his breeding herd. But now he was close to the turning point in his operation. Instead of growing his business further, he was soon going to start cashing in. The demand for beef in the eastern cities was high, and prices were better than he had believed possible. He was set to capitalize on the bonanza. He was counting on it. He'd borrowed money to convert his small log cabin into a real ranch house, never doubting his ability to pay back the debt.

The summer of 1886 was hot and dry. Grasshoppers plagued the arid land, sucking juice from the grass, flying up from the ground with each footfall of man or beast. The grazing was sparse, and was worn sparser still by the constant treading of cloven hooves. The hay crop was poor.

By July, the creek was barely more than a trickle with a few stagnant pools evaporating fast in the heat. The cows stood forlornly in the mud, trying to strain moisture into their mouths.

In the corral, the horses licked the bottom of the water trough. The windmill blades spun in the constant breeze, but when Jeb turned on the pump, brown water fizzed into the trough. It reminded him of the Coca-Cola he had bought at the drug store in New York City — a delicious drink that they said was good for your health. The thought made him thirsty.

Jeb fed hay to the horses sparingly, not wanting to use the forage that he had set aside for winter, but figuring he had no choice. Even so, Paint and the others chewed trees in the dry riverbed, stretching upward to snatch off curled crisp leaves, then circling the trunks with their teeth and stripping the bark as far as they could reach. Jeb knew the trees would not recover. They would die and their roots, which had stabilized the riverbanks and held back the blowing soil, would rot away.

By August the cattle were bawling piteously. They pawed at the ground, kicking dust into the air. They ate roots. They munched weeds. They devoured thistles. They chewed anything! Yet their ribs stuck out more each day, and their hides stretched tighter over jutting hipbones.

And the dry soil swirled in eddies. Day after day. Night after night.

A scant two inches of rain fell that entire summer. A quarter of Jeb's herd perished. They died of thirst. They died of starvation. They died when wolves attacked them. They died when vultures pecked them.

And their bones were bleached white in the merciless sun.

In September it rained, turning the grass a little greener. The surviving cattle and the horses ate non-stop.

But winter came early and was to be the harshest in living memory. Paint still had her summer coat when the first snow fell. She tucked her tail and tried to use the other horses as windbreaks, but they were all equally restless — jostling to reach the warmest position in the middle of the herd. They aggravated one another until one of them got nipped or kicked. Then they would all go racing across the paddock.

During the five years that Paint had been with Jeb, she had worked her way up to being boss mare, so when the petty squabbles started, it was her job to re-establish order. She would chase the others, pinning her ears and tossing her head. They would clamp their tails, fling their heads high, and bolt away to safety. But a strong-willed gelding with white-rimmed eyes would often challenge Paint. She would react instantaneously and terrifyingly, her neck fully stretched, her teeth bared, her tail swishing over her back. The challenger would veer away and keep his distance.

At last, with the hierarchy of the small herd

re-established, the horses were content to play together to keep warm, rearing and bucking, nipping and prancing, snorting puffs of air. Then, with heaving sides, they stopped to get their breath. Steam rose from their bodies, and before long they were shivering again.

The horses grew winter coats quickly. Paint's was as thick as a bear's, with plenty of loft to trap warm air between her skin and the sub-zero air. By November, when the winter really set in, she was so well insulated that snow didn't even melt on her back. It settled on her like a blanket, transforming her into a white horse.

Jeb still rode Paint on the range, checking the cattle. She had become his favourite horse, fast, agile and smart. But as the snow deepened it was harder and harder for Paint to break the trail. She tired easily, sweating under her heavy winter coat. Jeb allowed her to stop and catch her breath, but he never let her stand for long. He would urge her on, not wanting her to get chilled.

By December the cattle were hungry. They pawed through the snow, trying to reach the grass, but the snow was deep. The fat they had gained in September and October had melted off by December. They were burning muscle.

Jeb sent out a horse-drawn sleigh piled with hay, but the exertion of pulling the sleigh through deep snow drenched the horses with sweat. When they returned to the corral and relaxed, the sweat froze on their bodies and chilled them to the core. Jeb knew he would lose valuable horses that way. His hay supply was dwindling, too. Thanks to the grasshoppers and the summer drought, he didn't have enough to last even through a normal winter. And this winter was turning out to be the harshest on record.

Paint picked up on Jeb's anxiety. She could tell from his tense movements in the saddle and the sharp pitch to his voice. He no longer interacted with her as he had in the past. She sensed his inability to watch out for her safety, and to be her leader. Instinct kept her on the brink of challenging him for the role.

Jeb decided to bring the herd closer to the homestead. It would be easier to feed them, although the food wouldn't last long. But he couldn't stand by and watch the animals starve, not when he had a little hay that might keep some of them alive until the spring.

Most of the cowhands had moved on, but Chuck remained to help bring in the herd. So the two men and the two horses headed out to bring in the cows. Long before they reached the cattle, Paint smelled wolves. Her muscles tensed and her heart began to race. A short while later, Jeb saw their tracks. It concerned him, too. But unlike Paint, he was not fearful for his life. He had never known wolves to attack humans. He was scared for the safety of his herd, and for the profit that the wolves were stealing. He was angry at the thought of losing a single valuable animal to them. The summer drought, the cold winter, and now the wolves; it seemed that everything was against him.

Paint spotted the wolves first. She stopped and pointed her head with an intent stare. Jeb followed her gaze. He couldn't see the wolves initially, but he saw the cattle. They were not behaving normally. They were crowding together, then breaking away, making brief sorties, first in one direction and then in another.

"Wolves have got them spooked," Jeb said, urging Paint forward.

Suddenly all of the cows started running. Jeb knew it was just what the wolves wanted. Now they could separate the weak from the strong, the fast from the slow, the healthy from the unhealthy. They'd kill the weakest and slowest.

"My God," Jeb said, urging Paint into a lope, "I've never seen a pack this big. There must be twenty of them!"

Paint tried her best, but she couldn't lope for more than a few paces. Her hooves sank into the snow and left her floundering up to her chest. A few bounds tired her. The cows couldn't race through the deep snow, either. They were labouring.

Jeb fired into the air, hoping to scare off the wolves, but they kept chasing the cattle. One cow was already on the ground with several wolves on top of her. Another was surrounded, a wolf clinging to her haunches as she spun. Jeb aimed at the wolves that encircled her, but his fingers were numb and his shot missed. He cursed, then fired again. The bullet whistled by close to the wolves and they loped away.

"Damn it! They'll be back now they've got a taste," Jeb said, nudging Paint toward the first cow, still twitching on the ground. The mare balked. Jeb wasn't in the mood to persuade her that there was nothing to be frightened of, and he didn't have the energy to force her somewhere she didn't want to go. He got off and approached the cow on foot, struggling through the deep snow. Paint was pre-occupied with the whereabouts of the wolves and wasn't expecting the explosion from Jeb's gun. It startled her, but she held her ground. She looked at the cow on the ground. It was no longer twitching.

The scattered herd had regrouped some distance away, but the cow that had been fighting so valiantly remained close by. She was gasping, and the snow around her had turned red. Paint could smell the blood. When Chuck rode up to her, the cow made no attempt to flee from him. "Want me to finish her off?"

Jeb nodded.

Chuck reached for his revolver, took aim, and fired.

Paint had been staring raptly at the wolves. They were not far off, watching. The gunshot jerked her attention back to the cow, which collapsed heavily into the stained snow.

"Let's get the rest of the herd back home," Jeb said.

But the cattle had been badly spooked and they wanted no part of being rounded up.

"Can't you see we're trying to help you!" Jeb

yelled, blowing warm air down his gloves in an attempt to bring his frozen fingers back to life.

By the time the daylight started to fade, the cattle had become even more ornery, and Jeb and Chuck were exhausted, discouraged, and cold. They had no choice but to abandon the herd.

"Dumb cows," Chuck muttered.

As they headed for home, Paint turned her head from side to side, keeping watch on the wolves behind her. Shadow-like, they slunk back to the carcasses as soon as Jeb and Chuck began to ride away. They didn't wait for the two men to be out of sight.

CHAPTER FOURTEEN

In January a warm wind blew across the plains. Hope surged in Jeb's heart. But it was a chinook, lasting only long enough to melt the surface of the snow. Then the temperature plunged again, freezing the meltwater into a thick crust of ice on top of the snow. Jeb tried to ride Paint through it. For a few steps she slithered on the surface, then her hooves broke through and she plunged into the soft snow, ice shards cutting her legs.

Jeb knew that the cattle would be having the same problem. He wondered if they had the strength to dig through the ice crust to reach grass.

He felt frustrated. He could do nothing to help them!

The horses didn't move from the small area close to the barn where their manure and urine warmed the ground and their trampling hooves kept it clear of snow and ice. Despite the most frigid temperatures they had ever experienced, they didn't race around the paddock as they often did to keep warm in cold weather. They wouldn't risk falling on the ice. Instead, they huddled together. And with warning nips and kicks they squabbled for ownership of the hay that Jeb threw to them.

Spring came eventually, but it did little to gladden Jeb's heart. He rode Paint through the slushy snow, hoping to find survivors, but as the snow receded, carcasses appeared. Paint didn't like it any more than Jeb did. She veered away from a group of cows that were leaning into one another, propped against a snowbank, still frozen stiff. Jeb could feel her heart racing under the saddle. He finally persuaded her to walk past the macabre sculpture, but she eyed them suspiciously and gave them a wide berth, snorting in fear.

She stopped abruptly and backed up at the sight of a lone pair of horns poking through the snow. She spun and tried to bolt for home at the sight of a bloated cow on its back with all four legs pointing skyward. And she balked at the carcasses that tumbled down the gully in the powerful meltwater, piling up downstream: a dam of twisted bodies.

Much to Jeb's amazement, surrounded by the horror of death, he found the miracle of new life. The surviving cows were calving! Most calves were born thin and weak, and some were born dead. But a few survived.

The stench of decay hung heavily in the air. Jeb counted his losses. About sixty percent of his stock was dead. And more than ninety percent of the expected calves.

As the carcasses rotted into the earth, the reek of death faded. Jeb breathed a sigh of relief that winter was finally over and that the spring grass was already fattening up his surviving cows. The bad weather and the wolves had robbed him of all his anticipated profit, but he still had more stock than he had originally started off with five years ago. He'd be able to keep going. Unlike many others who had nothing left to pay their loans.

Banks were foreclosing on mortgages. Ranchers were giving up, walking away, leaving everything behind: horses, equipment, their dreams. It was a great opportunity for an ambitious rancher to increase his assets. But Jeb couldn't figure out a way to do it. The reality was that he could barely hold onto his own land. He'd need to sell some of his precious surviving cattle at the end of the summer just to pay his debt and stay in business.

Jeb's survival as a rancher depended on the grass. And the grass depended on the rain. Jeb felt sure that rain would come.

He was wrong.

No rain came. The melting snow was the only moisture the grass had that year. By June the short-cropped green carpet was already turning brown and the water level in the creek was dropping. There was no hay crop.

In previous years, Jeb had sent animals to slaughter in late September, after they had fattened on the summer's grass. But this year he rounded them up in June, thinking he'd cash in while there was still life in them. Other ranchers were doing the same. The market was flooded. The price was half of what it had been the previous year.

Jeb was becoming increasingly worried. The horses were thin, their ribs protruding from dry coats. He couldn't even sell Paint and the others. All of the ranches were going under. Nobody needed or wanted horses. Nobody had anything to feed them. Nobody had a cent to spend on them. He thought about setting them loose. Could they join a mustang herd, perhaps? But he knew they wouldn't survive. And the mustang herds had long vanished, maybe migrating into the foothills in search of food.

Jeb had become so attached to Paint he couldn't bear to think of her dying of thirst in what had become essentially a desert. It was kinder, he thought, to put a bullet in her head. He'd shot horses before. It wasn't nice, but it was the humane thing to do. It broke his heart, but, under the cir- cumstances, he felt he had no choice.

He caught her and led her to a quiet place behind the barn. He let his hands pass gently over her bony frame, exploring the places where black hair met white, his fingers following the swirling pattern, tracing the margins. He worked the tangles out of her mane with his fingers. He let his tears fall on her neck.

"I'm so sorry," he whispered, eyeing the spot he knew he must aim for, the place where death would be instantaneous. "Hold real still and you won't feel a thing," he said softly.

Tears blurred his vision, but he knew where to aim. He could do it blindfolded.

He tightened his finger on the trigger.

"For God's sake, Jeb, put the gun down!" Chuck yelled. "You can't shoot that horse. She's got a hold on your heart. Everyone knows that. Anyways, I got news! There's this man who's taking a string of horses up to Saskatchewan to a sale. He says they still have grass up there. And homesteaders need horses. He'll take your favourite mare. I already asked."

Jeb fell to his knees, his hands over his eyes, his shoulders heaving with sobs.

Chuck was stunned. He'd never seen Jeb cry. He'd never seen any grown man cry. He was embarrassed and didn't know what to do. "The border ain't far, Jeb. It'll take a week or two to get her up there, that's all. She'll have a chance."

Jeb wiped his grimy hands across his face "D'ya think she's strong enough to make it?" he asked.

"Sure. She's one tough little horse. If any horse can make it, she can!"

CHAPTER FIFTEEN

For days Paint plodded behind a rolling wagon. She was tied to a string of other starving horses, and was so tired that she could hardly put one foot in front of the other. She had no strength to jostle the others for dominance. She just let the wagon drag her along. Every evening when the wagon stopped, the man brought out oats and water. It wasn't much, but it kept her alive, barely.

When they arrived at the sales grounds in Saskatchewan, the same man led her into a pen. He filled a pail with water and gave her a pile of hay. She drank, but hardly touched the hay. Instead she lay down.

The man sighed, sadly. "I'll let you nap for half an hour, but then you have to get up and look lively. If you stay down there on the ground, nobody will buy you. They'll think you're at death's door!"

True to his word, the man came back in half an hour. "Get up, girl. Eat some hay! I didn't drag you up here just so you could end up in the slaughterhouse."

Paint didn't understand his words, but there was something in the urgency of his voice that spoke to her. She dragged herself to her feet and ate some hay. But she didn't have the energy to take any interest in the sale that was happening around her.

People passed by, but few stopped, other than to pity her, or dismiss her. None reached out in kindness to touch her. Except for one small boy. He reached his arm through the bars and stroked her face. His little fingers traced the outline of white that coursed down her nose and circled her eye. Normally Paint didn't like people stroking so close to her eyes, but she took a step closer to him, so he didn't have to stretch so far.

A man in clothes the colour of bare earth came alongside the boy.

He tutted. "Some people just don't take care of their animals. In England they'd be reported to the police."

A woman joined them. She wore a dress that came almost to the ground. It bore the faint imprint of dull flowers.

"A gypsy horse," she said, in a belittling way. "Do they have Gypsies here, too?"

The man didn't know the answer.

"Can we buy her, father?" the boy asked.

The man and the woman replied in unison. "No!"

"She's not what we're looking for," the man added.

The couple moved on and stared at a bigger and

heavier horse in another pen. They seemed excited about him. But the boy stayed with Paint.

"Tommy! Come over here."

The boy touched Paint's mottled nose, then raced off after the man.

Only a few buyers remained when Paint was finally led into the sales ring. She watched them. And they watched her. A group of three clustered together: the man and woman in the earthy clothes, and the same boy who had stroked her face.

"Poor thing's as thin as a rake," the woman said.

The man nodded in agreement. "I doubt she has the strength to pull a plow."

"Sure, she has," the salesman said. "These mustangs are always skinny, but they've got stamina."

"She's not what we need," the earthy man explained. "We're looking for a plow horse."

"You should have taken the last one! He was a good strong workhorse."

"The price got too high for us."

"Homesteaders, are you?"

The man in the earth-coloured clothes nodded and offered his hand. "Albert Cooper. And this is my wife, Margaret."

"Pleased to meet you both," the salesman said. "And this horse is *just* what you need! She's a real all-rounder. Give her a week or two to muscle up, then she'll throw her weight into the collar and make short work of the plowing."

The other buyers walked away, discouraged by Paint's weight and condition.

The boy tugged on his father's trousers. "Please, father."

"Tommy! We need a Shire or a Clydesdale, something bigger and stronger."

The salesman snorted. "They're hard to find! Everyone wants a big strong animal to pull the plow. There's two problems. First, they cost a lot! You can buy five regular-sized horses for the price of just one Clydesdale. Second, big horses have big bellies. I've seen them eat homesteaders out of house and home. You can't have a big horse taking the food from your boy's belly! On the other hand, this mustang won't cost you much to feed, she's accustomed to scrounging for herself. Give her some grass and before long you won't recognize her."

Albert and Margaret and Tommy were silent.

"Of course, some homesteaders use oxen," the salesman continued. "They're strong."

Margaret was horror-struck. She wasn't a peasant! She was an up-and-coming landowner!

Albert could just imagine how mortified his wife would be if she was seen driving into town on an oxcart.

"No," he said firmly. "We need a *horse*. But something heavier and stronger than this little piebald."

"This horse is the last one left," the salesman said. "There's another sale next month, so come back then. But get here early. The big horses sell fast."

Albert sighed.

The salesman sighed, too. "I'll be honest with you; anything that doesn't sell today goes to the glue factory. Doesn't seem anyone else is interested in her. So take her! Give me a buck to cover my costs."

Even though this horse was being offered virtually free, Albert still wavered.

"Please father, please."

The woman spoke now, too. "Albert! We can't let her go for glue. Let's take her. We can get a heavier horse later."

Albert knew that with horses it wasn't just the cost of buying them. He'd still have to feed the animal and care for it. And owning this half-starved piebald would reduce the chance of his money holding out long enough to buy a decent work-horse. But on the other hand, he needed a horse immediately, if only to pull the wagon loaded with his family and possessions to the homestead. If the poor animal could manage the eight miles there, it would be worth the dollar that the salesman was asking.

Heads bobbed and nodded, hands were shaken, and a deal was made. Albert took Paint's rope and she followed him out of the ring. She was too starved to be fretful. She didn't know these new people and they had no other horses. Loneliness normally made her unsettled and edgy, but a stupor had descended on her. The man passed the lead rope to the woman who held it nervously, then he boosted the boy onto Paint's back. The mare stood still, seeming to enjoy the sensation of the child's warm bare legs.

"She's really bony," the boy complained.

"That's because she's half-starved," Albert said. "If she's too uncomfortable you can always get off."

Paint had learned to recognize a smile on a human face, so she knew from the twinkle in Albert's eye and the shape of his mouth that the man was pleased.

"Walk her a few paces, Margaret," the man said.

The woman clucked at Paint and flapped the halter rope in her face. The horse remembered someone doing that long ago and, trying to oblige, she moved a pace backward in response. The woman panicked.

"Whoa!"

From the alarm in the voice, Paint realized that the woman was not a worthy leader, but the mare stopped moving backward anyway, because she was too weary to do anything else. The man took hold of the rope. He stood close, but didn't touch her. He waited for her to greet him first. She sniffed him lethargically. His hands smelled of salt and she licked them. When he scratched her under the jaw, she stretched in contentment.

"You like that, don't you?" he said, his voice low and hushed. "Poor old girl. You look really hungry. But don't worry. We're going to take good care of you! And in return I expect you to take good care of us. Especially our boy, Tommy. He isn't experienced yet with horses. So you and I have to teach him a few things."

The sound of his voice soothed Paint.

"Now, let's go," he said, walking purposefully

away from her, allowing the rope to lengthen and the distance between her to increase. Paint knew that he expected her to follow, and she did so without waiting for the tug on the rope. He seemed to be a trustworthy leader. The boy sat calmly on her back, twirling her mane in his fingers, his body moving gently with her footfalls, his bare legs relaxed against her ribs. It was familiar.

Albert led Paint toward the wagon surrounded by the mountain of things they had bought at the auction. She didn't balk at it. She was too tired to even bat an eye. She didn't object when the boy slipped off her back and the man gently put the collar over her head. Nor did she fuss when he backed her into the traces of the wagon and tied it all together with straps and bits of string. She even lowered her head into the stiff leather bridle, opening her mouth for the rusty iron bit. She stood, head down, while a pair of strong lads grunted to lift a metal contraption into the back of the wagon.

"This plow is heavier than it looks," one of them said, trying to manhandle it further in.

"Leave it right there," Albert said. "The closer to the tailgate, the better. It will be easier for me to get it out. We'll pack everything else around it. There's a sack of flour coming and some other things."

Margaret appeared with a box of food items and Albert wedged it into the wagon, along with a shovel, a garden fork, a cooking pot, a kettle, two blankets, and finally a mattress that they heaved to the top and tied down with string.

"Margaret! Tommy! Both of you sit up front," Albert said. "You can hold the reins if you like, Margaret, but you don't have to do anything. I'm going to walk alongside the mare. I think my weight as well as all the other things in the wagon will be too much for her. Anyway, until we can trust her, I'd rather be down here."

"What's her name?" Tommy asked.

"I don't know," Albert said, walking to Paint's head. "We can call her whatever we want. What would you like to call her, son?"

The boy chewed his bottom lip, deep in thought. Albert clucked, and the horse leaned into the collar as she had back in the days when she dragged the sling made from buffalo hide. But the wagon creaked and moved more easily than the sling ever had. It chased after her with surprising speed. But she was too tired to spook. She plodded along the rutted track toward her new home.

"In England, black and white horses are called piebalds," Albert said, getting back to the topic of naming the new horse. "But here, they're called pintos or paints."

"Paint! That's a good name, isn't it?" the child said.

"Yes, it is."

CHAPTER SIXTEEN

Despite their slow pace, the family reached the edge of town very quickly. Albert walked beside the mare, his feet moving in rhythm with Paint's hoof beats. The old wagon groaned with a life of its own, the wheels slotting into the well-worn ruts, the contents clattering when the wagon bounced over a bump or dipped into a hole. The procession kicked up dry dust that trailed behind them on the prairie wind. But the newcomers didn't see it. They didn't look back.

Close to town, the farms looked well-established. Farmhouses were built of stone. Golden wheat rippled and swelled in the breeze like the rolling ocean the family had so recently crossed. On one farm, men were swinging scythes, others were bundling the cut stalks, and piling them in stooks. In the distance the sun glinted off the metal of a good-sized barn, one that Albert could only have dreamed of owning in the past. Now it was part of his reality. He could barely wait to start farming his own land.

Soon the dwellings became smaller and more basic, sometimes just a shack, or a strange mound of grass that reminded the Coopers of England's ancient burial mounds. Some homesteads had nothing more than an overgrown cart track that seemed to lead into oblivion. Margaret started becoming anxious.

"We must have missed it," she called out. "Albert! Turn back. It can't be this far!"

"Another minute or two," Albert replied. But he, too, was getting concerned.

They came to another stone house. It was small compared to the ones in town, but it looked well-kept. There was even a name painted on a sign: HAMISH AND JEANIE MCDUFF.

Paint stopped of her own accord. She knew a horse was nearby; she could smell manure in the breeze, but even with her head held high she couldn't see him. She neighed, pricking her ears and straining to catch a reply, but there was none. She made an attempt to walk up the cart-track, but Albert corrected her and kept her straight. Margaret and Albert looked toward the house, hoping to see Hamish and Jeanie McDuff, but no one was in sight.

Wheat waved behind the McDuff house, but as the trio travelled farther along the road, they noticed that the ground sprouted mostly prairie grasses and wildflowers. There were no more houses. No signs of life.

They kept going.

The wagon ruts in the road became shallower until they were barely visible. Margaret gazed across the lonely, uninhabited landscape and her heart sank lower.

She looked down on the protruding haunches of the half-starved piebald, and realized that she was a travelling and displaced person, no better than the Gypsies that she despised. Like them, she was on the road. She looked at Tommy, grimy-faced and asleep in the crook of her arm, and at Albert, cheerless and stoic, trudging along in his worn work boots. She looked at the shabby, soiled dress that flapped around her bare legs, the once bright floral pattern barely visible. And she was almost envious for Gypsy life. Gypsies travelled in big family groups! Their wagons were brightly painted homes on wheels; caravans with chimneys! They played music, sang songs, danced. Their horses were well-fed.

"This must be it," Albert announced, bringing Margaret back from her thoughts.

She looked up, shocked to see that the road had completely vanished.

"Where did the road go?" she asked.

"It stopped. Ours is the last property at the end of the road, remember. There's the marker; that pile of stones."

"Where's the house?" Tommy asked, rubbing his bleary eyes.

Albert tried hard to put enthusiasm into his voice. "I'm going to build one, son."

Margaret looked around, hoping to see something other than sky and prairie. "Are you sure this is it? Perhaps we passed it already. Perhaps it was farther back, closer to town."

Albert recalled the conversation with the man

in the Dominion Lands office in Estevan. Self-important in his dark jacket, white shirt and tie, he had spread the big map out on the counter and pointed to the piece of land that he, personally, was allowing Albert to claim.

The couple had never seen a map like it before. Margaret was ecstatic because to her untrained eyes their homestead appeared to be really close to town. Albert had a better understanding of the scale, and he asked the government man to explain the meaning of the inked lines, and their *real* lengths in feet, yards, or miles. He had felt apprehensive.

"You should know that the land is marginal," the man had said, talking down his long nose.

"What's marginal?"

"Number one: the rainfall's not real reliable. But you have the creek. That's a big help." He pointed to a black line on the map that wiggled at an angle across one corner of the property. "Number two: there are more stones and rocks than most farmers like. But those stones are a great advantage. They'll make you a house!"

"We're going to build a brick house," Margaret blurted out.

"Of course you are," the man said.

His sarcasm was lost on Margaret, who, having realized that there was a general store across the road, decided to take Tommy shopping.

"How far is it from town?" Albert had asked.

"Eight miles."

Albert's heart fell. That was close to a two-hour

wagon ride one way. Four-hour return trip. Too far for Tommy to walk to school. Too far for Margaret to walk to the general store or the post office. "Can't I get land closer to town? We have a five-year-old who needs to start school!"

The man scoffed. "You should have come two or three years back. All the good places are gone. But as I said, you've got water. Think yourselves lucky — some folks have to start off by digging a well. And another good thing: wheat prices are high. There's been a drought down south. Crops all over America have failed. Bad for them, but good for you! It's all about supply and demand. Right now, demand exceeds supply."

He poked his finger at the square on the map. "This land here may not be the highest yielding land in the country, but remember there's a *hundred and sixty acres* of it! If you get even half of that planted in the next year or two, you'll make a fine living."

Albert knew in his heart that with just one horse and plow he couldn't possibly get that much land planted in a year or two. Ten acres was more realistic. Could he make a fine living on ten acres? He doubted it. Albert felt horribly trapped. This marginal land in the middle of nowhere was not what he had imagined, or hoped for. What's more, he knew that Margaret was going to hate it. And what was it going to be like for Tommy, growing up without friends, and no school close by? But what choice did he have? Getting to Saskatchewan had used up most of their funds. The remainder was earmarked for the essentials to see them through the first year, until a harvest brought an income. They couldn't afford to go back home! Margaret had always said that the offer was too good to be true. He hated that she might be right.

"It's this section or nothing," the Dominion Lands employee said, refolding the map in front of Albert's eyes. D'you want it or not? It's your choice, but I'd make the decision fast if I were you. Homesteaders keep coming. Another train arrives on Monday."

"I want it," Albert blurted out.

The man tapped the pen on the paper. "Sign here."

Albert signed. There was, after all, no going back.

"How do I find it?" he asked as he headed out the door.

The man had replied in a slow voice, as if he was speaking to a dull-witted child.

"Follow the road out of town. When it ends, that's you."

"Is it fenced?" Albert asked.

"You're getting the land for nothing! You expect it to be fenced?"

"No, I don't *expect* it to be fenced," Albert answered, trying to keep the irritation out of his voice. "I was merely wondering how to tell where the property lines are ... without fences, I mean."

"The surveyors have piled field stones on all four

corners. Your place is the end of the road. You can't miss it."

Margaret's shrill voice broke into Albert's thoughts. "Tell me this isn't it, Albert. Please tell me this isn't it!"

"This *is* it, Margaret. So for God's sake, stop nagging. I've had it!"

Albert stormed off, striding to the top of a faint rise, the only interesting feature of the landscape.

Margaret, unaccustomed to being spoken to in that tone, stayed on the wagon.

Tommy leaned into her, sucking his thumb.

Paint put her head down to graze.

From the top of the rise Albert stared out over the endless prairie. It rolled gently. There was no barn, no shed, no shelter of any kind. No trees. No neighbours. He had known that this would be the case. But the reality of the nothingness took time to sink in. Suddenly Margaret slipped her hand into his.

"It's the lack of people, rather than the lack of buildings," she said softly. "It frightens me. Who will help us if we need help, if we get sick, if we get hurt. There's no doctor for Tommy. We could die out here. Alone."

Albert felt a rush of protective love toward his wife. "We won't die! I'll take care of you and Tommy. I promise."

Margaret's emotions bubbled close to the

surface. She *needed* Albert to take care of her, but she wasn't sure that he *could*. She wasn't sure if *anyone* could. They had finally arrived, but she wanted to go home.

Albert held her in a hug.

She wiped her hand across her face and tried to smile.

Once, in what seemed to be a different life, Margaret and Albert had agreed on many things. They had agreed to come to Canada in hopes of a better life. Back in England, Albert had been a tenant farmer. He hadn't owned the land he worked, and he never would. In England, land ownership was for the wealthy, the titled, or the gentry.

Albert had seen a broadsheet about a place in Canada where you could get free land. A hundred and sixty acres! All you had to do was work it, build a homestead, and live there! Then, after a few years, the government gave you the deed!

Albert loved land. Even when he was a child, he would pick up a handful of earth and crumble it between his fingers, smelling it, savouring. The prospect of owning land in Canada lit a spark in Albert that refused to die. Pretty soon it was a blazing fire. He wouldn't let the opportunity slip away. Margaret had a vision, too, but hers was of a two-storey brick farmhouse. Anyway, they'd agreed to make the move.

They sold everything of value, worked at extra jobs, and with a loan from Margaret's mother they felt sure they had enough money to reach Saskatchewan and get on their feet. Albert would cut trees and build a log cabin to see them through the first year or two, but once the land was plowed and wheat was growing and money was coming in, he would replace the cabin with the brick farmhouse of his wife's dreams.

It took longer to get to Saskatchewan than Albert had ever imagined. He had no idea that any place in the world could be so far away! It was already the end of July when they arrived at the Dominion Lands office to make their claim.

And there were no trees.

CHAPTER SEVENTEEN

Paint spent most of the first few days eating. The grazing was ample and she ate non-stop! Albert was concerned that without fencing, she would run away, so he kept her hobbled, or tethered, telling her she could run free as soon as he stretched wire across part of the acreage.

Horses had always been a big part of Albert's life. Over the years he had worked with stocky Welsh cobs, enjoying their determination and pluck, and with Shire horses, loving the quiet nature of the gentle giants. He'd helped the village schoolteacher with a pair of rambunctious Shetlands who had minds of their own. He'd helped the vicar's wife with a Dartmoor pony who didn't like to pull a trap. He'd even worked with a flashy Arab that was a bit too skittish for the doctor's liking. But Albert didn't know anything about horses in Canada.

When he looked at Paint's slightly dished nose, her short back, and, now that she was feeling better, her head carriage and stride, he thought he could see a trace of Arab in her. But he'd never seen a piebald Arab. In his experience, piebalds and their brown-and-white counterparts, skewbalds, were heavyset animals. In England they were mostly seen pulling Gypsy caravans. Since Gypsies were not popular, it stood to reason that piebalds and skewbalds were never found in the stables of the gentry. Albert, in his lowly social station, had assumed this bigotry when it came to both Gypsies and their horses.

But Paint moved him. At first he was sorry for her. She was so thin and sad. But soon he loved her temperament, her personality, and even her painted appearance. With more time, he was sure she would blossom into a fine-looking horse.

Paint appeared to be content with life, spending her days sleeping and eating. But Albert became more anxious with every passing hour. He had never felt such pressure. Everything needed to be done immediately. The dread of winter was foremost in his mind. He had to be prepared or they would all starve or freeze to death. He was willing to work every day from dawn to dusk, but he was just one man. He could do only so much! Many tasks needed more strength than he alone could muster. Tommy was still too little and Margaret, well, Margaret was not much of a worker.

They'd been here for three days and had wasted each day! They were cooking on a campfire a few feet away from the wagon. They were sleeping on the mattress on the wagon floor, always ready to unfold the canvas and spread it over themselves should rain threaten. It didn't. Every day the sky was blue, and every night the stars twinkled. But Albert knew that the weather would soon change and that building a house was paramount, yet he didn't know how to start. All of his plans had been shattered with the realization that there were no trees to cut for a log home. The only trees on the entire property were scrubby things along the creek bed. They provided dead wood for the campfire, but they were certainly not suitable for building a house.

Albert recounted his money, hoping that by some miracle it would have multiplied into enough to buy lumber for a house. Of course it hadn't. He looked at the stones that erupted from the ground and knew they were a perfect building material, yet he had neither the time nor energy to dig enough from the ground and build a house before winter. Even a small one-roomed structure was beyond his physical ability.

Margaret's voice was urgent. It bored into his head like a woodpecker pounding against a tree trunk. "We need to go to town, Albert. Now! We've run out of matches!"

Albert wanted to yell in frustration. How could she not remember such an important item! They were so far from town! It wasn't like they could send Tommy around the corner to the village shop.

But what was the point of yelling at her? He hitched Paint to the wagon and they headed back toward town, stopping at the first cart-track that forked off the road to what they assumed was their neighbour's property. Albert took out his pocket watch. It had taken fifteen minutes to drive there in the wagon. Each member of the family looked down the track, each silently nursing their secret hopes. Albert hoped for a man to help him with things he couldn't do alone. Margaret hoped for a woman to talk with. Tommy hoped for boys to play with. Paint looked, too, hoping to see one of her kind. All of them were disappointed.

"It looks like a giant mole's been there," Margaret said.

"It's a sodhouse," Albert declared with a rush of understanding. "I'm going to see how it's made."

Albert guided Paint onto the hard-packed track. It was carpeted with stunted weeds and showed no recent wagon ruts or hoof prints. They passed a plow strangled by weeds, a frayed washing line strung between two leaning posts, and a lopsided outhouse with the door swinging in the wind. The place was abandoned!

Albert pulled the wagon up to the sodhouse. It was situated in a hollow, and looked as if it was built for little people, or as Margaret had said, a giant mole. Albert knocked on the door and called out a greeting, although he knew that no one was living there.

He pushed on the door. It didn't budge. He took a firm hold on the handle and heaved up and to the side until it he could jiggle it open. He ducked his head and entered. Mice scurried away in all directions, running up the walls and disappearing. He was glad Margaret had remained in the wagon. Tommy, however, was right underfoot, his eyes wide.

"Shush, don't tell your mother," Albert begged. "They're only mice! Nothing to be scared of, not for men like you and me! But your mum doesn't like mice. They frighten her. She thinks they'll run up her skirt."

Tommy giggled at the thought.

Surprisingly, Albert found that he could stand upright. The builder had dug down before using sod to build the walls, so almost half of the house was underground. The floor was packed dirt. There was even a stove with a chimney! And a small plank table with two benches. Albert needed all of these things. Necessity made him think that he should load them up into the wagon and make a quick getaway. Decency restrained him. He would make inquiries as to the whereabouts of the owners and see if he could beg or borrow the items, before he resorted to stealing them.

Margaret crept inside, cautiously. It was damp and dirty, dark and bare. She held her nose. But Albert was fascinated by the solid construction and the simplicity of the design. Rectangles of sod had been cut, each piece about two feet long, one foot wide and six inches deep. They were stacked, overlapping like bricks, to make walls. It seemed to Albert as if the roots had intertwined, holding the pieces of sod strongly together. The door frame was made of squared timber, but the roof was sod, laid over a dense framework of branches. In the dim light Margaret didn't see the cobwebs decorated with soil crumbs that had fallen from the sod roof. Suddenly they touched her face and grabbed her hair. She ran outside screaming. Albert followed her.

"It's horrid," she said, bursting into tears.

"It's been abandoned, that's why. Ours will be lived in! The stove will be lit. A lamp will be burning. It will be really cozy. This one is dark because it doesn't have a window, but I could put a window in ours. With glass!"

Margaret tried hard to look on the bright side. "Promise me it will be just until we get on our feet," she said.

Albert crossed his fingers behind his back. "I promise."

They pressed on toward town. After another fifteen minutes they came to the McDuffs' sign.

Again Paint stopped of her own accord. She knew that a horse had passed by recently. She neighed, but there was no reply.

"Can we live *here*?" Tommy asked, looking at the small stone house in the distance.

"No, but next year we'll have a house like this," Albert answered, trying to sound optimistic.

When Albert asked Paint to walk on, she sighed before obeying.

CHAPTER EIGHTEEN

By the time they reached town, Albert had planned the sodhouse in his head. He knew exactly what he needed to buy to make it a reality. He hitched Paint to the rail outside the hardware store and went inside.

"It's your lucky day, my friend," the storekeeper said. "I'm expanding the store! I just knocked down a storage shed out back to make room. I'll be re-using the good timber, but there are some pieces you can have for free, plus some sheets of tin roofing. They're rusted, but they still have a few years left in them. Come out back and see what you can use."

A small window caught Albert's eye. It was lying in the middle of the floor with smashed glass all around, but Albert knew how to fix it.

"You can take that door, too," the man said. "It's cracked right through, but you can have it if you want. And take all those small scraps of wood. You'll be needing something to burn to get you through the winter."

That reminded Albert about the wood stove in the abandoned sodhouse.

"Do you know who owns the vacant place, the one at the end of the road, right before mine?" Albert asked.

"Smitty's place? They left a while back."

"Will they come back?"

"Not a chance in hell!"

"So what happens to the land?"

"It will go to someone else, I guess. The homesteader act says you have to *live* on the land in order to get the title deed."

"What about the family's possessions?"

"Such as?"

"There's a wood stove I could use."

"Take it! If it helps you get through the winter. I'm sure old Smitty would be happy for you."

"Maybe I'll leave a note in case he comes back, telling him I've just borrowed it."

The man shrugged. "As you like, but there's no need. Believe me, he ain't coming back! Are there any trees on your land?"

"Along the creek," Albert replied, "but nothing too big."

"Don't cut them down. The roots hold the soil, stop it blowing when there's a gale. Stop it from washing away in a flood, too. Homesteaders have been cutting them. Big mistake! I understand that you all need wood and most of you can't afford to buy it. But once the trees are gone, it's damn near impossible to get them growing again, not with the winds we have around here. We've got to protect the trees! At least that's my humble opinion. Not that anyone takes any notice of me!"

Albert looked crestfallen.

"If I were you, I'd start collecting manure from that horse of yours."

Both men looked at Paint, who was sleeping in the traces of the wagon. Her bottom lip was flapping, her hip bones stuck out, and her ribs protruded. She looked as if she was well past doing a hard day's work.

"Making manure is probably the best thing that horse can do for you," he said with a chuckle.

Albert sighed. "We're saving manure already. For the vegetable garden."

"I don't mean that! I mean save it to *burn*! You folk from England have no idea how cold it gets here. You can stretch your firewood with horse manure. But it needs to be dry. We got the idea from the Indians."

"Indians?" Tommy said, wide-eyed.

"They used to burn buffalo manure — buffalo cakes!"

"Cakes? Yuck!"

Back at the wagon, Albert yanked the mattress on its side and tied it against the front, then he loaded in all the materials. Tommy helped. He gathered up all the scraps of wood, some of them barely bigger than sawdust.

On the way back home they stopped again at the abandoned sodhouse. Albert went inside to collect the table and benches.

"Margaret! There are some mason jars in here. I think they have stuff in them."

Margaret summoned the courage to re-enter the sodhouse. When she looked closer she could see that most of the jars were empty or had only a centipede curled up inside. But others, their shoulders covered with a fine layer of dry earth and their lids pitted with rust, appeared to be full.

She and Tommy carried them outside, excited about what the sunshine would reveal of their contents. A dozen jars of unspoiled beet, ten of pickled cucumbers, and two of purple-coloured jam. Even the empty jars made Margaret feel like it was Christmas Day. She would use them to can her own vegetables next year!

Albert in the meantime was manhandling the stove out of the house.

"Can you give me a hand, Margaret?" he asked.

"Leave it! Get someone to help you," she advised.

Albert's voice rose. "Get someone to help me! Who do you suggest? Do you see anyone around here? It's just you and me, Margaret. We don't have time for Tommy to grow stronger."

She sighed and summoned all of her strength. Together they hefted and wiggled the stove onto the wagon.

CHAPTER NINETEEN

Albert was finding the task of digging rectangles of sod much harder than he had imagined. The grass roots were deep. They were so tangled and thatched that, even though the new shovel was sharp, it took major effort to chop through the sod. Tommy was trying to help, but the boy's efforts made no difference whatsoever. In fact, he was getting underfoot and Albert had to make sure that his son's fingers or toes did not end up under the shovel. After several hours, Albert's hands were blistered, yet he had fewer than twenty sod bricks to show for his work. He needed hundreds, possibly thousands! The size of the house he had planned diminished in his mind as each hour passed. It was now down to a single room of ten feet by twelve. His blisters broke. He wrapped his oozing palms in clean rags and pressed on.

Paint neighed, her nostrils flared, her bony rib-cage trembling. With arched tail, she tried her best to prance forward, but the hobbles held her back. Albert looked up, too, his foot poised on the top of the shovel blade, his eyes following Paint's intent gaze. He saw a man on a horse in the distance. Albert suddenly realized how terribly lonely Paint must be. Horses, he knew, were herd animals. Living alone was not natural for them. He had been so concerned with his own problems that he had not been considering Paint's.

The rider waved his hand as he rode closer. With no introduction, and in a voice that was gruff, bordering on rude, he spoke three words.

"Need a hand?"

Albert chuckled. "Can you tell?"

Paint shuffled her hobbled legs close enough to introduce herself to the big honey-coloured Belgian horse. They sniffed noses amicably, then he rolled back his upper lip, inhaling the mare's scent.

The man slid off of the Belgian's bare back and surveyed Albert's work.

"Your horse can't pull a plow or what?"

"Yes, she can pull a plow ... I think."

"Well, what in heaven's name is she doing standing over there with her legs tied together while you break your back?"

Albert smiled at the man's sense of humour. "I didn't think we'd be able to plow the sod out neat enough to build a house."

"You can do it neat, and still be here in December, freezing your arse off with no shelter, or you can be a little less neat and get a roof on quick, before the snow flies. I can show you how."

"I'd be very grateful," Albert said, offering the visitor his rag-wrapped hand. "I'm Albert Cooper."

"Hamish McDuff. Pleased to make your acquaintance."

Hamish's hand was more like rough hide than human skin, and his fingernails were split and caked with dirt.

"This is Margaret, and my boy, Tommy," Albert said.

"And this here is Magnus," Hamish added, pointing to his horse. "Magnus seems to like the perfume your little mare is wearing today!"

The Scotsman didn't waste any more time on idle chitchat. He got straight to the point. "First things first. You need to plow a firebreak right round where you plan on putting the wee house."

Albert looked puzzled. "Firebreak?"

"Nobody told you about the wildfires?"

Albert felt like a fool.

"Fire sweeps across the prairie so fast you wouldn't believe it. But there hasn't been a bad fire for a few years, probably because it's been wetter than usual."

Albert looked at the dry grassland and thought he must have misheard Hamish, or misunderstood the man's accent.

"Last time a bad fire came through, it was five summers back; the first year we were here. The fire travels along the grass roots, see, so if you have a good swath of bare earth it gives you a fighting chance — to save your home, at least. We're short of time, so we'll do twelve feet now. We can broaden it in the spring."

Albert nodded his approval.

"And after you've been here a few years and have yourself some free time, like me —" Hamish stopped talking and roared with laughter. It seemed so out of character for the glum man that Albert was taken aback. "Then, in your free time," Hamish continued, "you can make a firebreak around the whole place, to keep the fire away from the wheat, too. But for now, show me your plow and I'll help you get started."

The two men walked to where Albert's plow was propped against a rock. Hamish tutted disparagingly. "Just a single share! If you had a double, you could plow twice as fast."

He looked at Paint, who was close to Magnus, both horses nibbling each other's withers. "I see you brought your lad's riding pony along for a holiday ..."

Albert frowned.

"That bonnie horse?" Hamish said, pointing at Paint. "She's not exactly a plow horse! Plowing your land with that wee thing will be like cutting the lawn at Balmoral Castle with a pair of scissors." Hamish scratched his bristling salt-and-pepper beard thoughtfully. "I could go home and come back with my plow, but we have nae time to waste. So we'll use this one, but I'll hitch Magnus to it. He'll make short work of things."

Hamish set to work with the harness, his fat, stiff fingers remarkably dextrous with the buckles.

"So where's this castle going?" he asked.

"Right on top of the rise here," Margaret replied, "so we get a good view all around." She rolled her eyes, trying to convey just what she thought of the view, but her meaning was lost on Hamish.

"You'll get the full force of the wind there, lassie. If I were you, I'd put it on the leeward side of the knoll. The wind comes mostly from the west, so I'd tuck her in right about here, into the hollow, so her west and north sides are protected."

Before long, Hamish was guiding Magnus in a large circle around the perfect house location. Albert had taken off Paint's hobbles, knowing she wouldn't run away now that she had company. She was following Magnus like a faithful dog.

Albert had never seen a Belgian before. He was impressed. Magnus had almost the same strength as a Shire or a Clydesdale, but without the height, and with a bit more agility. In no time the sod was being ripped and flipped. Some pieces came up in almost the perfect size to use as house-building material. Others were smaller and more crumbly. Albert trimmed the best pieces with his shovel. Before the Belgian was ready to start the next swath, Albert had hitched Paint to the wagon, and with Margaret and Tommy helping, he heaved the sod sections into the back.

By the time the sun was low in the sky, Albert had stockpiled enough sod to construct a house. He tried to express his gratitude to Hamish, but his words didn't do justice to the relief he felt inside. Hamish brushed off Albert's thanks. "I'll need *your* help one day."

The family stood waving at Hamish for a long time. Paint stood watching even longer. Albert had put the hobbles back on her. If not for this, she would have followed Magnus down the road. As it was, all she could do was neigh and hop a few inches at a time. Albert felt her loneliness. He walked up to her and scratched her neck, but it didn't help. She kept neighing and staring in the direction that Magnus had gone, everything in her body language saying that she wanted to go, too. For both their sakes, Albert hoped that Hamish would come back soon.

Paint was restless that night. She called to Magnus periodically, but he was out of earshot. Albert, Margaret, and Tommy, on the other hand, rested easier than they had for a while. They lay together on the mattress on the dirty wagon floor, looking up at the stars. So many of them, and so bright. The family talked about their new neighbour, laughing at the use of the word *neighbour* in this empty land. In England a neighbour lived a matter of yards from your door. Hamish lived far enough away to be in a neighbouring *county*!

Margaret was keen to meet Hamish's wife.

"As soon as the house is finished, we'll invite them both for tea," she said.

Albert was happy about that. He didn't know that secretly Margaret was worrying if a sodhouse would ever be fit enough to entertain in, and if the general store had Earl Grey tea.

The family was asleep when the wolves howled. Paint pricked her ears. She could tell the pack was a long way off. And she knew that the yips and howls were not hunting calls. The wolves were singing one of their social songs. Even so, Paint was nervous, instinct telling her to prepare to flee, or to strike out with her forelegs to save her life. But she could do neither. She was hobbled. Paint hopped toward the wagon and stood close to it. She had observed that wolves were more wary of humans than they were of horses. She sensed that the human presence would protect her.

Albert heard the wolves, too. He was unable to distinguish the meaning of their calls. He just knew that they were a threat to him and his family, and even his horse. He told himself to buy a gun the next time they were in town.

CHAPTER TWENTY

By morning Paint had settled to the serious business of eating grass and gaining weight. It took all of her time. She didn't even notice the Belgian until he was heading up the cart-track, with Hamish straddling his bare back. Paint neighed the instant she saw the big horse, and started hopping in his direction. Albert stopped working and looked up.

Hamish slid down Magnus's side until eventually his feet touched the ground.

"It's a long way up there!" he complained. "But at least you're nae short of a rock or two."

Albert looked puzzled.

"For me to stand on, when I have to climb back onto this beast!"

"Ah, yes, the mounting block! It's right there." Albert pointed to a rock with a relatively flat top not far from the edge of the cart-track.

"I can give you a hand for a couple of hours," Hamish continued.

Albert was relieved. He needed an extra pair of hands to help with the roof of the sodhouse.

Hamish started to unbuckle Magnus's bridle, then he stopped. "Do you mind if I turn Magnus loose? I don't want him treading on his reins, or grazing in his bit. Besides, he and your mare seem to be friends."

Albert had reservations. "Paint's in hobbles. She won't be able to get away from him if he decides to be boss."

Hamish guffawed. "Him? Boss? He's a big baby! He'd never hurt her."

Paint had been making her way toward them as fast as her hobbles would allow, and by the time Magnus was unbridled, she had arrived. The two horses touched noses and inhaled each other's scent. Paint nickered her greeting, but Magnus didn't answer.

"He never has much to say," Hamish commented. "He's like me! A man of few words."

As if to make his point, Hamish said nothing more as he and Albert strode across to where the sodhouse was emerging from the ground.

"You've done well, Albert, my lad," he finally said, after thoroughly inspecting the finished walls, complete with door and window.

Albert felt quite proud of himself.

Hamish looked at the mismatched scraps of lumber spread over the ground. "What's going on here, then?"

"I'm nailing these together, making them long enough and strong enough to span the roof. They'll support the sheets of tin."

"You're nae going to use sod?" Hamish asked in disbelief.

"Why use sod, when I have tin?" Albert replied, disappointed that Hamish wasn't thrilled with his design. "It will keep out the rain and the snow."

Hamish rolled his eyes. "You need sod for warmth, laddie! If you use tin, you'll be as cold as a witch's teat."

Tommy burst into an uncontrollable fit of giggles, which got both men laughing aloud, too.

"I have nae laughed that hard for a long while," Hamish said, wiping tears from his eyes.

"Believe me," Hamish insisted when the hilarity was over, "you need to keep every bit of heat inside these four walls. You don't want any of it going out the roof!"

Albert felt dispirited.

Hamish slapped him on the back. "Buck up! We can plow up more sod. It's the one thing you're not short of! And you can use the tin, too, to stop the sod falling down your shirt collar. It will be grand. But first, let's get these trusses organized. You've got to put 'em close together. A ton of snow will sit up there. You don't want the whole lot collapsing in January. A homesteader or two have been buried alive in these things, for want of a few more roof supports."

Albert was more than a little concerned.

"Don't worry, lad. These soddies last a long time if ye make 'em right. Mine's still standing and it's five years old!"

A few days later, Hamish returned, this time accompanied by his wife. They rattled up the road in the big farm wagon. Paint trumpeted a welcome, but Magnus once again refused to acknowledge her desperate greeting. Down by the creek, Margaret heard Paint's calls. She had just washed Tommy and had dressed him in slightly cleaner clothes. In haste to see what the excitement was all about, he scrambled up the bank. It was only a foot high, but he slipped, getting his palms and knees dirty once again. Margaret swore under her breath.

From the top of the bank the land was flat enough for Margaret to see the approaching wagon. She was thrilled that Hamish had brought his wife. She was pleased, too, that, despite his fall, Tommy was much cleaner than he had been earlier. She patted her strawberry blonde hair into what she hoped was a more presentable shape, tucking the stray strands behind her ears and poking them into the bun at her nape.

Then her thoughts flashed to what she would feed the visitors. With every rushed step toward them, she fretted more. She had no stove to bake a cake, only an open camp-fire. No chairs to invite them to sit and have tea, only the plank benches stolen from the abandoned soddie. She felt inadequate. But within seconds of greeting Jeanie, all of Margaret's insecurities were laid to rest.

"I've brought us a picnic lunch," Jeanie said.

"Everything we could possibly need, even mugs and plates! Hamish told me you're still camping out here. I remember what that was like. Goodness, we lived under the stars for our first summer, too. We had one cup and one plate to share between us. And precious little food to put on it, I might add!"

Margaret was trying to find the right words to express her relief, but the bubbly little woman gave her no time.

"Hamish is going to help Albert with the roof and I thought we could get to know each other. Then, when everyone works up an appetite, we can eat."

The men quickly got to work on the roof, Tommy doing his best to help. The horses grazed side by side. And the women walked down to the creek to sit in the shade under the trees. Margaret had always found it difficult to make new friends. Polite chitchat didn't come easily to her. She never knew what to say. But she didn't feel this way with Jeanie. They omitted the formalities, and the trivial things that strangers often talk about, and were soon sharing life experiences.

The two women were totally different. Jeanie was small, wiry, and strong, with short dark curls and tanned skin. Margaret was bigger in stature and softer in appearance. The sun had turned her freck-led skin pink, and her nose was peeling.

Jeanie was a hard worker who rarely let life get her down. When challenges came, she rose to the occasion. She never quit. Margaret on the other hand had always walked away from challenges, expecting first her parents, and then Albert, to deal with them. She was lazy by nature.

Under normal circumstances Margaret and Jeanie would never have become friends. But their circumstances were far from normal. After talking non-stop for over an hour they headed back to the wagon, which had moved since they last saw it! Hamish had not braked it, so Magnus had followed Paint around as she grazed, pulling the wagon behind him.

Jeanie climbed into the wagon, put on the brake, and started organizing lunch. The sight of a square biscuit tin brought Tommy running. It was painted all around with red tartan and on the lid were three sticks of shortbread. His mouth watered, and he couldn't help but let out a little gasp. He hadn't seen anything so good since he had left England.

"Oh, Tommy, I'm so sorry," Jeanie said. "It's nae shortbread in this tin." She opened the lid to reveal five hard-boiled eggs.

The men came off the roof, and soon everyone was eating. Apart from the eggs, there were boiled potatoes from Jeanie's vegetable garden, tossed in sour cream from Jeanie's cow and dressed with chopped chives from Jeanie's herb patch! And cold tea to drink. It was the best-tasting food that the family had eaten since leaving England.

"What can I do to repay you?" Albert asked when Hamish was ready to head home.

"Bring young Tommy down to visit us sometime.

It would warm our hearts to have a bairn around again."

"Have your children grown up and gone?"

Hamish sighed. "They've gone alright, but they never got the chance to grow up."

"Oh, I'm so sorry," Albert said.

"Aye, this place is a killer."

CHAPTER TWENTY-ONE

Paint wanted to trot all the way to the McDuff homestead. Albert kept reminding her to walk, but as soon as he released his grip on the reins she picked up speed again.

"She knows she's going to see Magnus," Tommy said from the wagon.

"You're right, son," Albert replied.

"She doesn't know where he lives," Margaret said, her tone indicating that she thought her husband and son were both mad.

"She certainly does," Albert said. "If I take my hands off the reins and let her go wherever she wants, I guarantee that she'll take us straight there."

Margaret sucked her teeth. Paint heard the noise, thought she was supposed to go faster, and broke into a lope. Everyone laughed. It felt good. As Albert had predicted, Paint turned off the road and trotted smartly down the McDuffs' track, neighing at full volume. If Albert hadn't pulled back on the reins, she would have gone right past the house and on toward the barn and paddock where Magnus was standing stock still, watching her. She stopped on Albert's insistence, but danced on the spot, tossing her head while the family climbed down.

Jeanie and Hamish were waiting out front to greet them, but no one could make themselves heard above Paint's neighs, so they decided to take the mare to the paddock and turn her out with Magnus.

Paint walked with such speed that Hamish had to jog to keep up, barely giving him time to point out the old soddie as they raced past. "That was our first home. We spent two years in that," he explained, puffing.

Albert unharnessed Paint, wondering if he could do better than Hamish, and build a stone house in the coming year.

Paint pranced into the paddock, neck arched, tail high.

"What a bonnie lass," Hamish said. "She came from mustang stock, for sure. You can see Arab in the way she floats!"

Albert was surprised. "Mustangs have Arab blood? How did that happen?"

"Christopher Columbus!"

Albert stared quizzically at Hamish.

"He brought the first ones to the New World. Spanish horse."

"Ah-ha!" Albert exclaimed. "Spanish horses have a lot of Arab blood."

"That's it. Some of 'em escaped, or were stolen, who knows … anyway, they went feral and thrived."

"Huh," Albert said. "You mean my scrawny little piebald horse is part Arab?"

Hamish nodded.

All five of them leaned on the gate, watching the horses for a while. Paint tore around the field, clods of earth flying from her hooves.

Albert smiled. "She hasn't been able to do that at my place. She's hobbled all the time, or tethered, because I haven't got fences yet."

Magnus trotted after Paint as if he was in a parade, his knees lifted high and his thick neck arched. Then, when Paint was huffing for breath, she sidled up to Magnus and nibbled his neck under his flaxen mane. He responded by nibbling hers.

"What will you do with her in the winter?" Hamish asked.

"I was hoping you could give me some advice about that," Albert replied. "I had planned on building a barn, or at least a shed, but with no lumber, it's pretty hard. I hear that mustangs are hardy and can live outside. What do you think?"

"Up here? With no shelter? She'll die. Wild mustangs have the sense to head to where it's warmer, but we get too much snow. The grass is buried. They can nae get enough to eat."

"Can't they dig for it?" Margaret asked.

"Aye, but digging takes a lot of energy, and the grass does nae have much goodness when they finally get to it. Anyway, your mare can nae dig with hobbles on!"

"I was forgetting that," Albert said. "What

should I do, Hamish? I can't let her freeze or starve."

"You can leave her here with me. It seems she and Magnus are best friends, and I've enough hay."

"But how will we get around?" Margaret asked. "We'll need to get to town occasionally for supplies. And what if someone gets sick?"

Hamish guffawed.

"I said the same thing our first year," Jeanie replied. "It takes a winter to learn that you can't go anywhere when the snow really sets in."

"Aye, that little horse with her skinny legs and wee hooves won't help you! She'll sink to her chest in snow. And she certainly won't be able to pull the wagon through it. There are days when even my Magnus can't get out. And look at the size of his feet!"

Margaret was stunned. "So you're saying that once the snow falls we're stuck in a sodhouse in the middle of nowhere ... with no transport ... for months?"

"Naw, not for the first few snowfalls. They generally melt a bit, so you can still get around. But by November or December ..." He left the thought unfinished.

Margaret looked horrified. And Albert's head dropped into his hands.

"So I have to get all the supplies in by then?" he exclaimed. "Everything to see us through until the spring? Everything?"

Jeanie sighed almost apologetically. "The first

year is the hardest. Let's go inside. The coffee should be ready."

"So have you moved everything into your new home?" Jeanie asked as soon as they all entered the house.

Margaret snorted. "That took less than ten minutes! All we have is a mattress, the table and benches we took from Smitty's place, and a packing box we brought from England."

Jeanie laughed out loud, her eyes crinkling at the corners. "I remember those times," she said. "So tell me, where in that sodding castle of yours did you make the bedroom, and where did you make the kitchen?"

Margaret laughed at the coarse humour that seemed so out of place with the compassion that welled in Jeanie's smiling eyes. Together, their laughter took hold like a roaring steam train, turning into snorts that sent both women to a new level of hilarity. And then, before she knew what was happening, Margaret was sobbing. For the first time since saying goodbye to her mother, she felt understood.

The men stood by, pretending not to notice as both women dabbed their eyes on handkerchiefs, Jeanie's fingers working her square of thin grey cotton into a ball.

"This wee rag has seen a lot of tears," she said, melancholy tingeing her voice. But she didn't dwell on it. She set her face into a smile. "Let me show you around. Hamish made everything," she said proudly. "He built the house, too."

Hamish interrupted. "*We* built the house. I could nae have done it without Jeanie. Homesteading only works when a man has a good woman working alongside him."

Margaret felt a pang of guilt.

"The walls didn't cost me a penny," Hamish added. "Every one of these stones was free! Fieldstone is the best crop around these parts. They come up by themselves! You pick 'em and drag 'em off the field, thinking that you've got every last one, but next spring, darn if there's not a whole new crop! And you've got to go stone-picking again."

Hamish took the broom, and touching Tommy gently with it on both shoulders solemnly said, "I hereby knight you Sir Thomas — Chief Stone Picker at DunEagle Castle!"

"Where's that?" Tommy asked.

"That's your home, silly. And if I were you, I'd appoint your ma to be your assistant stone picker."

"She's a mother!" Tommy said, "Mothers don't do things like that."

"In this country they do! So shall we dub her and make her your assistant for all time?"

Tommy nodded, almost biting his knuckles with excitement.

"You do it, then," Hamish said, giving Tommy the broom and helping him recite suitable words. "On behalf of Queen Victoria — in the Dominion of Canada — I dub you Lady Margaret, *Arse*-istant Stone Picker —"

Tommy exploded with giggles. Tears of laughter poured down Margaret's cheeks.

Hamish reached for a bottle and poured a finger of golden liquid into a single clay goblet. "And now we must toast our new dignitaries." He took a sip before offering it to Albert. "Whiskey, made from potatoes. Tell me what you think."

Albert almost choked on the fiery liquid. "Good," he said as it rolled down his throat, the warm glow spreading out into his body almost instantly. "Very good."

"And a wee drop of Saskatoon berry wine for the lassies ... and, of course, young Tommy."

"To friends!" Jeanie said, raising her glass.

"To friends!" they chorused back.

"Funny, eh?" Hamish observed. "In the old country the Scots and the English don't make friends."

When the men took Tommy outside to catch Paint and hitch her to the wagon, Jeanie handed Margaret a large parcel wrapped in newsprint and tied with string. "I thought these might fit Tommy. There's no sense me keeping them here. I'd be pleased if you would use them." There were tears in her eyes.

"I'd be honoured," Margaret replied.

CHAPTER TWENTY-TWO

Albert didn't realize he'd forgotten to hobble Paint until the next morning when he discovered she was gone. He cursed at the top of his lungs, furious at his own inattention to detail. He was about to head off along the road on foot to see if he could find her when Magnus appeared, pulling the wagon. Hamish and Jeanie sat up top, and Paint cavorted alongside, trying to get Magnus to play with her. But the Belgian was stoically concentrating on his work.

"Look who spent the night at our place," Hamish called out. Albert was indescribably relieved to have his horse back safe and sound, but she was acting strangely. She kept swinging her rear end toward Magnus and backing up into his face! Magnus poked his nose into the air, rolled back his top lip, and sniffed.

Hamish winked at Albert. "Shame Magnus has been fixed. The poor old fellow doesn't know what he's supposed to do!"

They all indulged in ribald laughter at the expense of the two horses; Magnus restrained in the traces of the wagon, Paint prancing around boldly in front of him.

"Now you're here, Hamish," Albert said, "will you come back to Smitty's sodhouse with me? There might be a few more things we can scrounge. I've got my eyes on the outhouse! And Margaret wants to have another dig through the old vegetable garden, in case there's something edible."

"Sounds like a grand idea," Hamish replied.

Albert backed Paint into the traces of the wagon, and in no time the two families were heading along the road, Magnus leading and Paint keeping as close as the wagons would allow.

When they arrived at the deserted homestead, the men and Tommy took the horses and wagons farther into the property, looking for anything that they could use, leaving the women forking through the old vegetable garden. It had gone wild. The weeds were waist high, but a few things had survived or reseeded themselves. Hidden underground they found potatoes, carrots, and a few beets. They also found a tomato plant with ten tomatoes in various stages of ripeness and a patch of garlic.

The men returned with a haul of dead wood that they had gathered from under the trees along the creek. Paint was still trying to entice Magnus, squealing at him, flicking her tail and shifting her weight back and forth from one hind leg to the other. Magnus was unimpressed.

Everyone ate a ripe tomato, juicy and warm from the late-summer sun. Then, after debating the most efficient way to dismantle the walls and roof of the outhouse, they set to work. They pried it all apart and carried it to the wagon until all that remained was the throne; the wooden seat that covered the hole in the ground. There was no smell. It had dried up long ago, but Tommy pegged his nose in disgust and wandered off to explore.

Behind the soddie, he discovered two things he didn't recognize. They were identical and each had a curved wooden frame that stood almost as tall as he was. Between the frame was a mesh of rawhide. They didn't weigh much, so he yanked them free from the weeds and carried them to his father.

"What do you have there?" Albert asked.

Tommy shrugged.

"Have the two of you never seen snowshoes?" Hamish asked.

They hadn't.

"These are much too big for you, Tommy. They're made for someone about your da's size. They'll help him stay on top of the snow, just like a rabbit. In fact, I think that with these on his feet, your da could hop along to my place for a visit."

"I want some, too," Tommy begged, "so I can come and visit you."

"It sounds as if we should all have a pair," Albert said, taking a good look at them. "D'you think we could make some, Hamish? It's just wood and rawhide strips."

"We can get the rawhide, but the wood needs to be curved right. I'll see what I can find at home."

CHAPTER TWENTY-THREE

The first snow fell in early September. It melted in the afternoon sun, but there was a rawness to the wind that had not been there before. It sent Albert and Margaret into a frenzy of preparations.

By late October the ground was covered with snow. Albert decided that it was time to take Hamish up on his offer of looking after Paint for the winter. He bridled the mare and rode her bareback down the road, loping part of the way through the soft white snow. It was exhilarating. The sky was bright blue, a shade he rarely saw in England. The air was still, and the landscape sparkled with a brightness that dazzled him. The heat from Paint's body warmed him. He wondered if he was doing the right thing, taking her to Hamish's, but he felt he had no choice. The hobbles had prevented her from straying until now, but with the arrival of snow, she needed her freedom to dig down to the grass. He knew for certain that if he took off the hobbles and gave her a choice, she would hightail it to Magnus in a flash. And that made the decision easier for him. He would miss her, though. He'd grown fond of the mare.

Paint had no reservations whatsoever. For the last five minutes of the journey she was neighing at top volume, the sound vibrating through her bare back into Albert's body. Finally Magnus answered her.

Hamish had heard them coming and was waiting at the barn. Magnus was waiting, too, pressed up against the gate. Hamish shooed him away, so that Albert could lead Paint in. She was impatient to have her bridle off, tossing her head so that the leather crown got stuck over one ear. She pulled away, dragging it from her face. Finally free, she squealed, bucked high into the air, released a massive fart, and galloped flat-out across the paddock. Magnus arched his docked tail and followed her, lifting his legs in a spanking trot.

Hamish laughed. "That's as fast as he can go!"

Albert felt confident that Paint would enjoy the winter.

"Come on into the barn and take a look around."

Albert had once hoped for a house and barn like Hamish's, but recently he had learned that everything was much more difficult than he had ever imagined. Hamish recognized the look on Albert's face. "Don't worry. You'll have a place like this in a few more years," he said.

Albert peered into the first of five stalls. Reddish-brown hens strolled around, pecking and clucking, while others sat in nesting boxes. A good-looking rooster surveyed them from his perch.

"They stay here for winter and I feed 'em corn," Hamish said. "But the rest of the year they have the run of the place. They catch grasshoppers and eat all sorts of things."

Hamish moved to the second stall. "And this is Betsy. Jeanie milks her twice a day." Albert stroked the face of the small Jersey cow, her long tongue flicking out to touch his hand.

A black steer occupied the next stall. "This is Betsy's calf. He's six months old. He'll be butchered in the spring, right before the next calf arrives."

"He looks more like an Aberdeen Angus than a Jersey," Albert said.

"Aye, that he is! There's no point in breeding Jersey to Jersey, not if you want something with meat on it. There's a man a couple of farms down with an Angus bull, so we leave Betsy there for a couple of days. He's got a fine-looking stallion, too! A Canadian. Jet black, not too big, but stocky and strong."

Albert didn't know there was a Canadian horse breed.

"They've been here since the French first came. A really good type for homesteaders. Broad through the chest, lots of bone, you know what I mean?"

"Sounds perfect for the plow," Albert said.

"Aye! And they're easy keepers, too. He and Paint would make you a fine horse."

Albert was surprised. "Paint? I think she's too old. Judging by her teeth, I'd say she's more than fifteen. Perhaps sixteen or seventeen."

Hamish guffawed. "Too old! Did you see her strutting around like a tart a few months back? Damn it, that mare was in heat. I don't care what her teeth say. She is *not* too old!"

The other two stalls were empty.

"When the weather gets really bad, Paint and Magnus will come in there. I'll leave them out as long as possible. They prefer it, quite honestly, as long as they have lots of hay. There's a lean-to shelter on the south side of the barn, so they can get out of the worst of the weather. If we get freezing rain, or wet snow, and their coats get wet through to the skin, that's when they feel it the most. But as long as their skin stays dry, they don't seem to mind being out in cold temperatures."

Albert glanced up.

"There's a big loft up top, for hay."

"How did you build this, Hamish? It's bigger than the house!"

"Jeanie and I built the walls out of stone, just like we did the house, and once we had a couple of good wheat harvests, I was able to buy the timber. Then something grand happened. Everybody for miles around came here for two days; men with their hammers and saws, women with food. I didn't even know most of 'em! Twenty-four people, all told! And we got a roof on real quick. Since then I've been out to help build a few more barns. When you're ready to build yours, I'll spread the word and we'll do the same."

Albert's spirits soared.

"See what I have for you," Hamish said, leading the way and proudly showing Albert two pairs of snowshoes. "I think these will fit Margaret, and these will fit Tommy."

Albert was overwhelmed. "I don't know how to thank you!"

"Albert, my friend, my motives are purely selfish! With these snowshoes, you'll have no excuse for not coming down to see us during the winter. We get a bit lonely, see. And we've enjoyed having you about these last few months." Hamish was close to choking up, but he pressed on, giving instructions. "Choose a bright, clear day when there's no wind, otherwise your skin will freeze. You can lose fingers, or toes, or ears to frostbite, so be careful. You'll have to go in the front — to break the trail. The others can follow in your footprints, so it's easier for them. And it's much easier going home for the same reason."

Albert shook Hamish's hand, once again feeling that his words of thanks were inadequate to convey what he felt inside.

That evening when Hamish entered the paddock, dragging a skid filled to overflowing with loose hay, Magnus trotted up as usual, helping himself to a mouthful as Hamish dumped it onto the ground. Paint waited respectfully until Hamish was out of the way, then she kindly asked Magnus to move, so that she could eat first. If the big Belgian had been more attentive, he would have noticed Paint's ears flick back and her nose stretch forward. But he was busy eating. She charged at him. It was rapid and violent, her bared teeth connecting with his rump and pulling out a tuft of fluffy golden hair. Magnus veered away as quickly as he could, and stood a few yards off, chewing on the hay he had escaped with. It was only after Paint had pushed her nose through the pile, flipping hay in all directions and eating the choicest morsels, that she allowed Magnus to move in next to her and share.

Hamish laughed. "Women!" he said, to no one in particular. "Bossy, aren't they?"

CHAPTER TWENTY-FOUR

Paint's black-and-white coat grew thicker and denser as the days grew shorter and colder. The abundant grass in August and September, coupled with Hamish's best hay, had enabled the mare to regain her lost weight and put a layer of fat over her ribs. This helped keep her body heat in and the cold air out. Hamish, wisely, didn't coddle the horses at the onset of winter, knowing that to put them in the barn would slow down their ability to acclimatize to the cold. The lean-to on the south side of the barn had always protected Magnus from the worst of the weather, and Hamish was confident that it was all Paint would need, too.

But Paint didn't like the shelter. She couldn't relax in it the way Magnus did. From the moment of her birth on the plains, the sky had been her roof. No walls had ever contained her. Her excellent vision, coupled with the wide open space, allowed her to see danger from afar, giving her time to flee. In the shelter she couldn't keep a lookout, and the noise of the wind howling around the corner made her think that a predator was lurking nearby. Survival instinct would send her galloping into the field.

One day in November an icy rain began to fall. Magnus was dry under the shelter. He was accustomed to the noise of rain and sleet drumming on the roof. But it unsettled Paint, and she bolted into the open and waited there, too nervous to seek cover. Before long, her coat was soaked and her skin was wet. Chilled to the bone and miserable, she flattened her ears and took a run at Magnus, nipping him on the rump and driving him out into the rain, too. She goaded him into a canter with more nips and kicks, and they made several circuits of the field. It warmed her a little, and took the edge off her temper.

Magnus watched her carefully, waiting for her pinned ears to flop sideways, her pinched nostrils to relax, and her angry eyes to soften. Then, tentatively, he made his way back to the shelter and found the best corner, out of the wind. She didn't join him. She lowered her head, rounded her back, and clamped her tail so that some of the rain dripped off her flanks, keeping her belly dry.

Just before dark, Hamish came out to check on the horses and found Paint shivering violently. He led her to the barn, walking into a stall and expecting her to follow. But it was dark inside the stall and she balked. Hamish didn't want a battle, so he tied her where she stood and set to work with a mud scraper, shedding water in sheets from her sodden coat. She was irritable, not wanting to stand still, and calling nonstop for Magnus. He, for a change, answered.

So Hamish brought the big horse into the barn, too, and led him into his own stall. He noticed the new bald patch on Magnus's rump. "She's been bossing you around again, I see," he said, gently stroking the gelding's neck.

Hamish rubbed handfuls of hay all over Paint and eventually her violent shivering stopped. He carried fresh hay into the empty stall, and Paint followed him in, but as soon as he bolted the door, her head shot up in alarm. She peered over the partition to where Magnus was peacefully munching hay. The whites of her eyes were showing and her lips were pursed.

"Nothing can hurt you here, lassie," Hamish said softly. "You're safe."

But Paint couldn't relax. She was trapped, contained. Magnus was half asleep, untroubled by lurking predators. As leader, Paint watched out for both of them. She rubbed her chest back and forth on the dividing wall, trying to get out. She chewed the top edge of the railing, then paced around the stall. But there was no escape.

Eventually, lulled by the sound of Magnus's steady breathing, she nodded off, too.

When Hamish came in the morning, Paint tried to barrel past him the instant he opened the door of the stall. But Hamish held his ground, refusing to be pushed around, and she waited until he released her into the field. Then she bolted, kicking up the slushy snow, bucking in all directions, neighing for Magnus to join her. When he trotted up to her, she pinned her ears and faked a charge, just to let him know that she was still the boss.

🐎

Back at the Cooper homestead, Albert, Margaret, and Tommy were settling in for the long Saskatchewan winter.

On cold and blowing days they went outside for two reasons only: to fetch fuel for the stove, and to use the outhouse. They were glad they'd placed it right outside the door, and they laughed at their earlier concerns that it wouldn't look very good, or smell very good, so close to the house. There was no one out here to look at it. And nothing smelled in this cold.

As the days grew shorter, the wind chilled the air to a level of cold the English family had never imagined. Air froze in their nostrils and snow squeaked underfoot. When Albert returned to the warmth of the little sodhouse after each brief outing, he found himself silently thanking Hamish for helping him build a home. It was crude and small, but it kept them surprisingly warm. If not for Hamish, Albert knew that they would be struggling for their lives.

With every bowl of Scottish porridge they ate, every piece of hot Indian bannock, every Canadian pancake sprinkled with sugar, Margaret thought of Jeanie. For she had shown Margaret how to cook these thing without the oven she was accustomed to. Even when they played a round of cards, or helped

Tommy write his ABCs on the slate, they talked about their new friends, for Jeanie and Hamish had given them all of these things.

On nights when Albert slept soundly, not waking even to stoke the stove, the light of day revealed intricate ice ferns on the inside of the window. But as soon as Albert coaxed the fire back to life, the patterns melted, running in little rivulets down the pane, and soaking into the greyed wooden frame. Then, with the stove devouring a fresh supply of wood and dry manure, the heat in the soddie became almost unbearable. Tommy and Albert stripped down to their underdrawers, and Margaret shed her heavy cardigan, flapping her hands across her flushed face, threatening to open the door.

Eventually Albert learned how to keep the stove burning slowly.

With little to do, the Coopers often sat staring out of the small window. They had never seen such large flakes of snow and at first they were mesmerized. They were shocked, too, the first time they saw the snow rising from the ground and heading skyward in spiralling eddies. And many times they debated if it was actually snowing, or if the same old snow was being whipped back up by the wind into a fresh frenzy.

After one particularly heavy snowfall the window was completely covered by a drift. The darkness in the soddie made Margaret think she was in a tomb, being buried alive. Albert opened the door, shovel ready to repel the snow that avalanched inside. Then he cleared a path to the outhouse and the woodshed, and carefully scraped the snow from the window glass. When daylight crept back into the dark house, Margaret breathed a sigh of relief. The window had become her lifeline. It was her link to the outside world, even though the outside world was far away.

CHAPTER TWENTY-FIVE

Over the wintry months, Tommy began to learn his arithmetic in two ways. One was by counting pickles: "Ten pickles in the jar, we eat three, how many are left?" Margaret soon realized that there were not enough pickles for them to eat one each day. So she cut them in half. And then in quarters and eighths. This was how Tommy learned fractions.

The second and more exciting way of doing arithmetic was by counting down the days to Christmas. This had become a daily ritual ever since the first flakes had fallen in September. Each day Tommy took out the only pencil they possessed and, under the guidance of his father, ceremoniously marked off the day in the notepad that Margaret had made into a calendar. Then he counted the remaining days in as many ways as the family could think: How many Mondays? How many hours? This proved to be difficult for *all* of them.

The countdown to Christmas forced Margaret to think about the season more than she should have, and the thought of spending it away from her parents was upsetting. Her musings took her back to the village church, the focal point of Christmas activities. Margaret had never enjoyed church. She went each Sunday because that was what people did on Sundays. Besides, church justified the expense of a new dress or hat. It was also an opportunity to catch up with village gossip and news, such as who was courting, who was pregnant, who had just given birth, and who was dying.

The loneliness of the prairie, however, caused Margaret to remember church more fondly.

Albert had always enjoyed church more than Margaret. He sang in the choir and had also been a bell ringer. Both these activities gave him the opportunity to go to the pub after practice and have a quick pint with the men.

The village church was built in the Norman era, dating back to William the Conqueror of 1066. It was made of stone, had a square bell tower, and was always cold and damp inside. Despite the prayers and hymns of the congregation, Margaret found both the building and the services to be oppressive. After giving birth to Tommy, church had been even more of an ordeal for her. It was fine when he was little. She remembered being pleased beyond words to show off Tommy dressed in the blue matinee jacket that her mother had knitted.

But by the time Tommy turned two, going to church became more difficult. He wouldn't sit still. He slid back and forth along the oak pew, climbed on it in his shoes, and when Margaret tugged at him to sit down, he swivelled around to make funny faces at the people behind them. And he couldn't keep quiet! His voice echoed around the stone church. Sometimes his antics got a quiet giggle from other worshippers, but more often than not Margaret felt the shame of condemnation that she couldn't control her son. And on more than one occasion she dragged him to his feet, a little too forcefully, and marched him down the aisle, her head lowered to hide the flush of embarrassment.

However, Margaret had to admit that on Christmas Eve at midnight something magical happened in that ancient Norman church. Even Tommy felt it! Lit by hundreds of candles, the grey stone walls shone like gold and a warm glow touched the faces of the working poor and the landed gentry alike. With gentle strains of *Silent Night, Holy Night* rising to the vaulted ceiling, shivers always rippled down Margaret's spine. She had felt love. She had felt peace.

As Margaret gazed through the sod house window at the falling snow, she said, "I was just thinking about last Christmas, Tommy. What do you remember?"

Tommy answered right away. "Presents! I got soldiers."

Margaret smiled, remembering the six toy soldiers made of lead that Albert had bought for Tommy.

"And I remember going to Granny and Granddad's house," Tommy continued, laboriously practising the letter *T* on his slate. "Granddad gave me a sip of Christmas spirit."

"He didn't!" Margaret shrieked, remembering her father's custom of serving sherry on Christmas Day.

"It was horrid," Tommy said, spitting out the words. "Granddad said it's the reason that everyone is happy on Christmas Day. He said it's why you get giggly, Mum, and why everyone talks so much and so loud. Can we go to Granny and Granddad's this Christmas?"

"No," Margaret replied sadly. "They live too far away." Tears welled in her eyes and her voice started to quiver. She'd been putting on a brave face for a long time, but now her sobs turned into a wail that shocked Albert and frightened Tommy. It was more than sadness. It was a desperate loneliness. A deep ache for her mother. She'd felt this way once before — for her sister. Back then, anger had erupted to drown out the sorrow: anger toward the man on the runaway horse who had trampled her little sister. Now, Albert was in line for that same rage. He had taken her from her home and family. It was *his* fault. It was *his* idea — not hers. She wanted to spit all of these things in his face, but the grief came from a place so deep that she was unable to speak. She couldn't catch her breath.

Albert tried to comfort her, to find out what was wrong. But all Margaret could do was wail. Eventually, like a storm passing, calm returned, but she had given herself a headache and was exhausted. She went to bed, stifling the anger she still felt toward Albert.

CHAPTER TWENTY-SIX

Playing in the freshly fallen snow helped to keep Tommy cheerful. He liked nothing better than hurling snowballs at his father, ducking and diving with glee as Albert lobbed them back. The anticipation of Christmas also seemed to keep Tommy in good spirits. But as November gave way to December, both Margaret and Albert worried that there was so little to give their son. Margaret was secretly knitting him a hat, scarf, and mittens in his favourite colour: red. And Albert was trying to carve a whistle, but he wasn't getting on well. The lamplight was too dim to do the job safely. He was becoming frustrated.

Tempers were frayed.

The Coopers were getting on each other's nerves.

Twenty days before Christmas, Tommy accidentally tossed their one and only pencil into the stove along with the kindling. It was the breaking point.

"What have you done, you stupid boy!" Albert yelled.

Tommy burst into tears and hid behind his

mother, clutching her skirt as she rose to confront her husband. "Stupid?" she screamed. "How dare you call him stupid! We live like moles because of *you*." Her lip curled in disdain. "*You* brought us here. It's all your fault! *You* dreamed of having your own land. It wasn't my dream, and it wasn't Tommy's." With that, Margaret burst into tears. "I want to go home," she sobbed.

Albert reached out to touch her shoulder, but she pulled away from him. "I hate living like this, like worms tunnelling underground. I can't bear it any longer. The dirt! The dark! The cold!"

"I'm sorry," Albert mumbled.

She didn't seem to hear him. "Take us home, Albert," she insisted. "Take us home now!"

Albert knew that trying to reason with Margaret at that moment would get them nowhere. She was past being reasonable. He grabbed his outerwear and left the house. Lacing on his snowshoes, he started off down the track toward the road. Snow was falling, driven sideways by the wind. But he didn't care.

Margaret had no idea how much time had passed when Tommy started complaining he was hungry. She looked out the window. The snow was blowing fiercely and it was getting dark. She lit the lamp and started to worry. A few moments later, without waiting to put on her coat, she rushed out the door. She couldn't see Albert. She couldn't even see the track, let alone the road. It was all obliterated by blowing snow. It hit her hard in the face, stinging her skin. She pounded on the outhouse door, then threw it open. One glance inside set her heart racing. He wasn't there.

She walked a few paces into the driving snow. "Albert!" she yelled.

"Daddy!" Tommy shouted, slipping his hand into hers and gripping hard. Margaret looked down at him. He had no coat on and was shivering. So was she. Guiding the boy back inside, they quickly put on their outerwear before venturing back out.

They stood together in the growing darkness and yelled at the top of their lungs, but their voices were carried skyward in the swirling eddies of wind and snow.

Even with the snowshoes, Albert was sinking deep into the soft, fresh snow. Each step took great effort. He stopped to catch his breath and looked back. The sodhouse had vanished. A bolt of panic brought him to his senses. *I could die out here*, he thought. He had to get home. The dread of confronting Margaret's anger faded with the knowledge that he was responsible for both her and Tommy. If he froze to death in a blizzard, they, too, would die.

Albert turned and retraced his steps as quickly as he could, but soon all the tracks had disappeared, buried under the drifting snow. He stopped again, his breath ragged from exertion and anxiety, and told himself to calm down. The house was not far away. He sniffed the air, hoping to catch a scent of smoke from the chimney, but there was nothing. He turned to try and get his bearings, but the movement of the driving snow caught him off guard and he suddenly became disoriented. He didn't know which way he had come from, or which way to go. His eyes were playing tricks on him, too. He was blinded by the enveloping whiteness, lost. Exhaustion swept over him. His senses told him that his situation was serious, yet his panic faded. He just wanted to lie down and rest. He collapsed in the soft snow, praying that God would help him get home.

Margaret left the lamp burning brightly in the window, the wick turned high, then she and Tommy went back out into the storm and walked a little farther from the house, glancing back constantly to check that they could still see the light.

Suddenly, the wind dropped, and the snow stopped.

They held hands and called out.

"Albert?"

He heard his name. It came to him as if in a

dream. He wondered if it was an angel calling him. He waited, peacefully.

"Daddy!"

Forcing his aching muscles to move, Albert dragged himself toward the sound of his son's voice.

When Albert crawled into view, Margaret and Tommy rushed to him and helped him to stand. One on each side, they managed to get him into the house, to the warmth of the woodstove. He was confused and barely able to speak. Margaret had never seen frostbite, but she'd heard about it, so she checked his fingers and toes and ears and nose, all the places she knew were vulnerable. Three toes on one foot were white, not pink like the others. She melted snow in a pan on the stove to make a warm footbath, and she sat with him all night, topping up the warm water.

By morning Albert had the feeling back in his toes. He hugged Tommy and apologized for calling him stupid. Then he apologized to Margaret. "You're right, Margaret. It's *my* fault that we came here. If I could take you home right now, I would. Please believe me. But we can't leave in this weather. We have no choice."

"I know, Albert. I know." She sighed and said no more.

"We're in this mess together, Margaret. It's the only way to survive."

CHAPTER TWENTY-SEVEN

Without the pencil, the Coopers struggled to keep track of the passing days. But they all thought it must be close to Christmas. Albert guessed the big day was seven days away and he announced that as a fact, feeling sure that baby Jesus wouldn't mind if they celebrated his birth a few days early or a few days late.

Albert had been whittling small pieces of wood into characters from the Nativity. He'd started with the animals. Three sheep and a donkey were already finished. There was little difference between the donkey and the sheep: all had four legs, a head, and a body, but Tommy rubbed chalk on the sheep to give them white fleece. Mary and Joseph were whittled next. Under Tommy's imaginative direction, Mary rode the donkey up onto the wooden box in front of the window. The box, originally a packing case that had stored their few possessions on the voyage from England, had become a shrine to Margaret's former life. She laid her mother's white crocheted doily on the top and the lamp was placed on the doily, leaving just a neat frilly edge visible. Despite the constant dirt from both the stove and the sod walls, Margaret ensured her shrine was clean and symmetrically arranged each day.

Now Mary and Joseph invaded this sacred space. With Joseph on one side of the lamp and the sheep on the other, the blessed virgin awaited the arrival of baby Jesus. Unfortunately neither Mary nor Joseph were very steady on their feet and frequently fell over.

"Too much Christmas spirit," Albert joked, giving Margaret an urge to taste the warm glow of her father's sherry, quickly followed by an even stronger urge to cry.

Tommy woke early on Christmas morning, but it wasn't until daylight filtered through the window that he could see baby Jesus had arrived. There were no shepherds or wise men, Albert's enthusiasm for the project having waned. But Tommy was happy to use his toy soldiers as substitutes.

Albert launched into the only Christmas carol he knew that seemed suitable under the circumstances: *"In the bleak mid-winter, frosty winds made moan ..."*

Margaret joined in, warbling along with him: *"Earth stood hard as iron, water like a stone. Snow lay falling snow on snow ..."* She thought that the writer of this old English Christmas carol must have spent a winter in Canada.

Tommy was pleased with his gifts. Wrapped in the new scarf and hat, his mitten-clad fingers explored the three holes of the whistle, creating piercing screams that Albert hadn't anticipated. Within ten minutes, Albert wished he had carved the boy a wooden gun instead.

Margaret had saved some salt pork especially for the big day, so they feasted. She sent up a prayer that there would be enough food to last them through the winter.

Boxing Day dawned sunny, clear and still. It was the perfect day to make the long trek to the McDuffs. As soon as the Coopers had eaten their porridge, they strapped on their snowshoes and set off. They followed one another in single file as Hamish had suggested, Albert in front breaking the trail, Tommy in the middle, and Margaret bringing up the rear. The effort kept them all warm, in fact too warm. Sweat was running down Margaret's back by the time the McDuffs' house finally came into view.

Albert had sold his pocket watch back in October to help buy winter supplies, so it was impossible to tell exactly how long the trek had taken, but he estimated about two hours. That made him anxious about the return trip. He didn't want to overstay the visit and run the risk of getting caught in the dark.

Hamish and Jeanie were thrilled to see them.

Jeanie clapped her hands together and grinned

from ear to ear. "What a grand present, to have you here with us for Christmas dinner!"

"Christmas dinner?" Margaret exclaimed. "But Christmas Day was yesterday!"

"Naw, it's today," Hamish announced, smiling. "Merry Christmas!"

The smell of roast chicken wafting from the kitchen confirmed that the McDuffs were right. It was indeed Christmas Day. And a feast was in the oven.

"We would never have imposed if we'd known," Margaret said.

"It's no imposition, my friends," Jeanie insisted. "There's more than enough food. And we're delighted to see you. It's been so long. We have so much to talk about."

Soon the women were peeling extra potatoes and carrots and chattering non-stop.

Albert and Tommy were keen to see Paint, so after Albert drank one of Hamish's hot toddies and Tommy had a mug of warm milk, they went outside with Hamish.

The sight of Paint brought a broad smile to Albert's face. She sauntered to the gate when he called her name, nuzzling his hands, gently prying open his fingers to see if they held anything edible. Tommy took off his woollen mittens and allowed her to lick the salt from his hands. The Belgian wanted to approach him, too, but Paint wouldn't let him. She flicked back her ears, telling him to stay away. He ignored her gentle request and tried to butt in, so she swung her rump around, cutting him off and raising a hind hoof as a stronger warning. Magnus backed up out of range and waited.

Albert was horrified. "I can't believe she did that!" he said to Hamish. "She's the visitor here and she treats him so badly."

Hamish shrugged. "She's a mare!"

"Does he ever fight back?" asked Tommy.

"Naw. He seems to like being put in his place! She's taken a few chunks out of his arse." Tommy couldn't stifle his giggles. "Not enough to break the skin, mind you," Hamish continued, "she just pulls out clumps of hair. That's the worst of it."

"So you aren't upset?" Albert asked, hoping that Hamish was not mad at either Paint or him.

"Naw!"

Albert was relieved. "She's a beauty now, don't you think?" He looked at Paint's thick velvety coat. "Look at the guard hairs under her belly, and under her chin. They must be three inches long! She's really rounded, too."

Hamish looked at the mare thoughtfully. "You're right."

CHAPTER TWENTY-EIGHT

During Christmas dinner, Hamish had given Albert a good idea. As soon as they got back home he set to work, whittling wood into sharp pegs, then hammering them high up into the dry sod walls. With a well-worn bedsheet hanging from the pegs, the dark, dirty wall became a clean, white wall. It lifted their spirits. Margaret was able to hang things from the sheeted wall, items that needed to be kept clean such as the enamel mugs they had each carried attached to their belts all the way from England. Encouraged, Albert made more pegs, and all manner of things were lifted from the packed dirt floor to be hung against the white wall.

Over the next few days the sun shone and the snow sparkled, and the wind wasn't too fierce. The Cooper family went outside to play, all three of them flopping on their back in the snowdrifts and flapping arms and legs to see who could make the best snow angels. They had snowball fights and they built snowmen: more and more of them as the weeks passed. Soon a parade of rotund, frozen men with twigs for mouths and horse manure for eyes kept vigil on either side of the pathway to the door.

Chilled, they returned to the warmth of the soddie, hanging their damp clothes and sodden mittens on the wall pegs. The wet wool steamed, giving off the smell of clammy sheep.

As the days grew longer, Margaret began to think that spring must be just around the corner. But still the winter dragged on. In England, spring was a lengthy but gentle season starting as early as January, with snowdrops pushing their delicate heads above ground. Throughout February and March, each week brought some new marvel: crocuses, daffodils, leaves on the trees, vividly green grass, cherry and apple blossoms. The birds courted, sang, and nested. Lambs and calves were born. Nature was bursting with new life. But on the Saskatchewan prairie, it was April, and everything was still sterile. Dead.

Just when Margaret felt she couldn't stand the gloom any longer, rays of sunlight shone through the window, making the dust motes sparkle. They also highlighted a fine layer of wood ash on the doily and dirt on the pane of glass, but instead of going into a cleaning frenzy, Margaret sat in the small patch of sunlight, eyes closed and heart filled with gratitude that Albert had thought to make a window.

"It must be spring!" she said, hopefully.

Warmer days started to melt the surface of the snow, but cold nights turned it into sheer ice. Twice a day Hamish and Jeanie strapped spikes to their boots so they could safely reach the barn to tend the animals. The horses stayed close to the shelter, walking gingerly, avoiding injury by not taking any unnecessary steps or by chasing each other. Not that Paint had been chasing Magnus much recently. She seemed content to stand around, resting a leg or nodding off. Even if Magnus dared to nibble what Paint considered to be her hay, all she did was flatten her ears and glare at him, and he would quickly back away. Hamish noticed that Magnus was getting thinner and Paint was getting fatter.

A few miles down the road, the Coopers pretended to be ice-skaters, gliding in their work boots, Tommy falling on his backside in fits of giggles. Albert became impatient to start plowing his land in preparation for planting. But under the first half-inch of mud, the ground was still as hard as iron. The shovel bounced off it, sending jarring waves of pain down his forearms. However, as the days turned into weeks, the sun seemed to move with breathtaking speed back toward the house. The land was warming fast. The snowmen they had built became nothing more than sodden twigs and horse manure floating in puddles. And the creek became a raging river, swollen to three times its original size and swirling with brown meltwater. Heeding the McDuffs' dire warnings about the danger of getting swept away, Albert wouldn't let Tommy or Margaret close to it. Then, suddenly, the ground thawed: one day it was frozen solid, the next it was soft. Albert walked down to the McDuffs' to get Paint.

As soon as he saw the mare, Albert knew she was in foal.

"Hamish!" he yelled. "I thought you said Magnus had been fixed."

"It wasn't him!" Hamish exclaimed. "Magnus *is* a gelding. There's no doubt about that. I think your mare had her way with that black Canadian stallion I was telling you about."

"But how? When?"

"That night she escaped, remember? Back in August, when she came down here. I reckon she paid him a visit first."

Albert looked horror-struck.

"Look on the bright side," Hamish said with a chuckle. "You saved the stud fee!"

"But I've got all that land to plow! I need her to work harder than she's probably ever worked in her life. I can't expect her to be a plow horse in this condition."

Hamish shrugged. "Mustangs are tough. She'll give you more than you expect."

Albert rode Paint home, his legs stretched around her enlarged belly. Hamish had promised to come up later with a wagonload of hay to keep her going until the pasture was green. But even so, Albert was worried.

After a few more days, the worst of the mud had dried and Albert hitched Paint to the plow. He started doing what he had waited so long to do — working his own land.

Paint threw her weight into the collar and Albert manhandled the plowshare that jumped and kicked through the deep grass roots. It wasn't easy for either of them. It required strength. English soil had been broken by others, way back in history. This was different. It was virgin grassland.

After the long winter cooped up in the sodhouse, the family felt reborn. They were all happy to be outside in the spring sunshine, breathing the fresh air and working. Tommy and Margaret both rose to the occasion, becoming the best stone pickers they could possibly be, Tommy keen to show his father how strong he was, and Margaret determined to become a good homesteader wife like Jeanie.

Paint wasn't so keen on working, though. She was soon winded with the effort of pulling the plow. Albert knew he should give the mare more time to rest, but he needed the land plowed! His family's survival depended on sowing wheat seed while the soil was moist from the snow. He looked at the small patch of land he had plowed; then, as his eyes scanned the acres of untouched grassland, he became frantic.

When the McDuffs arrived with Magnus, Albert breathed a sigh of relief. In fact, he was overwhelmed when he realized that the Scotsman had rounded up other homesteaders from the area, too. Over the course of a week, several families arrived with teams of horses and picnics to share. They spoke mostly English, or English with a Scottish accent. But one family spoke no English at all! Hamish said they came from the Ukraine. Albert was stunned, and grateful for their generosity. Margaret was thrilled to have some women to talk to. And Tommy, previously a shy child, was soon playing with the other children. It didn't seem to matter to him whether they spoke English or not.

Under Hamish's directions, the men and horses plowed north to south so that the prevailing wind would run across the furrows, not along them. Hamish had learned the technique from a Russian who had farmed on the dry steppes. It was the best way they knew of to lessen the amount of soil that was carried away by the wind.

The men plowed until their energy was depleted. The women and children worked hard, too, hefting and dragging fieldstones into piles, then feeding and watering both men and horses, energizing them to work on through the warm afternoon. With close to forty acres of land broken, and a sun that was getting hotter by the day, the men returned to work on their own farms. Albert's bumbling words of thanks were dismissed.

"I planted winter wheat in the fall, so I was at a loose end!"

Albert felt sure that no homesteader could ever be at a loose end.

"We didn't want you to go under like Smitty did. If we'd all helped him a little more, maybe he would have stayed."

"The wife needed to get out after the winter and see some other folks!"

The Ukrainians smiled, shook Albert's out-stretched hand, patted him on the back, and spoke words that Albert couldn't understand.

It was quiet once the last family had left. Albert looked over his plowed acres and was satisfied. Long, almost straight furrows converged as they disappeared into the distance. It wasn't plowed as well as an English field. There were clumps where the soil hadn't been broken down enough. But Hamish had said that for this year it was sufficient, and that the clumps were a good thing! The wind wouldn't whip the topsoil away as easily as if the surface was harrowed to a smoother and finer texture.

The next day the Cooper family started seed-ing. All three spread across their land in a straight line. In almost hypnotic rhythm they reached into their bags, grasped a handful of wheat kernels, and with a sweeping motion let it fly through the air in an arc. It was monotonous. It was mesmerizing. Nobody spoke. All three were lost in their own world.

Paint had a few days' rest.

When the seeding was done, Albert looked over his land and was content. Thanks to the neighbour-ing homesteaders, more land had been started than he had even hoped for. He wondered if the profit from forty acres of wheat would be enough to build a stone house and a barn, buy a cow, and erect some fencing. He hoped so.

CHAPTER TWENTY-NINE

After the land had been seeded, the Coopers planted a vegetable garden. Then Albert bought fence posts and wire on credit, promising to pay when the harvest came in. The family worked together fencing a paddock to keep Paint and her expected foal in, and the wolves out.

The vegetable seeds in Margaret's garden hardly had time to germinate and poke their tender tips above the soil before a late May frost killed them. Margaret replanted.

The forty acres of plowed land was transformed into a vivid green carpet. It was the most magnificent sight Albert had ever seen.

The dozen pullets they had bought in the spring started laying eggs, but a hawk picked off one of the hens. A fox took three others.

Albert bought lumber, again on credit, and built a shelter with a hay storage area. They called it a barn.

A dry spell in June stunted the young wheat, turning it yellow, but Albert felt sure it would pick back up when the rain came. And in the meantime the dry spell was perfect for haymaking. Lads from the town arrived and helped. Rain fell right after the hay was safely stored. Albert counted his blessings. The rain revived the wheat, which shot up overnight in the damp, fertile soil.

Rabbits ate the lettuce. Albert shot a few; they made good eating for a family deprived of meat.

Grasshoppers attacked the wheat, but the surviving hens chased them, running and jumping and feasting, then laying eggs with bright yellow yolks.

Tommy waged war on a multitude of bugs that the family didn't recognize, including huge cutworms, which sliced through the stalks of their tomato plants like razor blades. He collected them in mason jars and fed them to the chickens, his hands toughening from the occasional peck.

Albert felt that he was making good progress. The next thing the family needed was a cow. Margaret thought they should borrow more money and get one straight away, but Albert felt the weight of what he already owed.

"As soon as the harvest comes in," he promised.

And then, in July, Paint went into labour. Albert and Margaret both knew that the mare's time was close. She was restless and her swollen udder was leaking milk. Albert started fretting. Paint's belly was enormous. The Canadian breed was significantly heavier than Paint, and Albert worried that the foal was big and the birth would be difficult. He was fearful of losing the mare.

Albert made a bed of hay in the shelter, hoping

to keep the mare close by, but Paint had other ideas. She ambled into the middle of the paddock, swishing her tail. She lowered herself cautiously to the ground, but a few seconds later she heaved herself up.

"She can't get comfortable," Margaret said anxiously.

"What's that?" Tommy asked as a tiny pair of hooves appeared.

"Hopefully the front legs," Albert replied. "If it's the back ones, we're in trouble."

Then a nose came into view.

"Thank God!" Albert said. "It's the right way round. They're supposed to come out like this, see?" He stretched his arms forward and tucked his head between his elbows, like he was diving into a water hole.

Paint decided to lie down again, and the foal's forelegs and nose vanished. But as soon as she was on the ground, they reappeared. Tommy watched, wide-eyed. Margaret held her breath. And Albert kept his fingers crossed behind his back.

They waited for what seemed like hours, but was really only a few minutes. Nothing happened.

Albert's concern was growing. He knew that horses foaled fast, and if they didn't, the chances were high that both mare and foal would die. In England, help would have been minutes away. But here, there was no help. They were alone.

Paint was making no progress. Dread started to fill Albert's heart. She was too old to be having a first foal. *But maybe this wasn't her first foal.* He reasoned that she had probably foaled many times before. That would make it easier for her.

Still nothing happened.

Albert began to panic. "I think she's going to need some help, Margaret. We'll have to pull, or we're going to lose her. Have you got those towels handy? We'll wrap them around the foal's forelegs for a better grip."

But before Margaret and Albert had time to get organized, Paint pushed one more time and her foal rushed out in a gush of fluid.

All of Albert's pent-up anguish came out, too, in one great sigh of relief.

Paint's head flopped wearily to the ground and she lay still. The foal struggled a little, kicking his long, spindly legs and tossing his head.

Margaret was alarmed. "There are membranes over its nose, Albert! It won't be able to breathe. You have to do something!"

Albert was calm. "It's best not to interfere. He doesn't need to breathe yet. The cord's still attached, it's nourishing him."

"It's a boy?" Tommy asked.

"Yes, it is," Albert replied.

Paint lifted her head from the ground and turned around to look at the foal. Almost immediately she started licking the membranes from the colt's nostrils, and he took his first breath.

Margaret gasped with joy, then started crying. Tommy was both fascinated and repulsed at the same time.

The mare got to her feet, the cord breaking at its weakest spot. For eleven months, mother and foal had been one, but now they were two. Paint set to work massaging and drying the foal, nickering softly, encouraging him to stand. The colt responded by lurching to his feet, only to tip forward onto his nose and collapse to the ground. He sat for a while, his muscles becoming stronger with each passing second. He tried again, this time making it up onto his long, wobbly legs. He stood for a second, then, very slowly, his legs began to slip out from under him, each heading off in a different direction until, once again, he was back on the ground.

Tommy giggled.

Paint was preoccupied eating the afterbirth and membranes, lapping up the birth fluids, devouring anything that carried the scent of birth, so for a while the colt rested. With the cleanup complete, Paint whinnied softly but urgently, pacing around her foal, anxiety crinkling the mottled velvet skin of her nose and lips. Instinctively she knew what her mustang ancestors had learned over the generations: predators would already be on their way, following their noses to an easy meal, and her offspring must be on its feet and able to run.

Paint nosed the colt hard, almost flipping him over. His soft hooves were already hardening in the dry air, and this time when he lurched to his feet, he stayed upright. He concentrated on lifting each leg, and took his first faltering steps, swaying like a stick insect on a blade of grass. Tommy held his breath, willing the spindly creature not to fall, watching as Paint guided him to her swollen udder.

Tommy, Margaret, and Albert all grinned broadly.

"What are we going to call him?" Tommy asked.

"Maple Leaf!" Margaret exclaimed. "Look. There, on his hindquarters." She pointed to a perfectly shaped white maple leaf surrounded by dark grey baby fluff.

"Huh," Albert said. "What do you think, son. Is Maple Leaf a good name?"

Tommy shrugged. "What's a maple leaf?"

"We saw lots of them when we were on the train coming out there, remember? They're Canadian trees. They don't grow in England."

Tommy considered this. "A Canadian horse with a Canadian leaf on his bum! I think it's a fine name."

Paint nickered ever so softly to her foal. It was a voice they had not heard the mare use before, and Margaret's face lit up.

"He's so little!" Tommy murmured.

"He'll grow to be much bigger and stronger than Paint," Albert announced.

"How do you know?" Tommy asked.

"He has big hooves for a baby. And enormous knees and hocks. They look out of proportion with the rest of his body, but he'll grow into them. He has a thick neck, too." Albert beamed proudly. "He's going to grow into a powerful horse, just what we need for working the land."

CHAPTER THIRTY

By the time Paint's foal arrived, the Coopers were just weeks away from the start of harvest. The stalks and leaves were turning from green to gold. And when the sun settled in the evening sky, a honey-coloured haze spread over the landscape that was beautiful to behold. Driven by the dismal prospect of another winter in the soddie, Margaret had spent every spare minute of the summer lugging field-stones to the site of her new house. She was already imagining herself in a sun-filled kitchen, cooking delicious family meals in a real oven. There was just one problem. They had no money to buy lumber for the trusses, windows and doors, or metal sheeting for the roof.

"As soon as the harvest comes in," Albert said again.

Teenage boys came from town to help with the harvest. Armed with scythes, they bent low, slashing the wheat stalks and felling them in a single swipe. Margaret and Tommy followed along, threshing the grain from the stalks and putting it in sacks. Finally,

Albert hefted the sacks into the wagon and drove the load to the mill in town.

Pride in his accomplishment vanished when he found out the going rate for wheat. More land was coming under the plow each year, he was told. Rain, followed by a hot, dry spell just before harvest time had produced a bumper crop. Supply exceeded demand. Albert felt that he was being cheated. When he argued, he was told that he might get a better price at the next town, and to go right ahead. The next town was twenty miles away. Albert settled. He had no choice.

Albert counted his cash. There wasn't enough to buy the lumber and metal sheeting for the roof, not after paying his debt at the hardware store and buying the supplies they would need to see them through the coming winter. Margaret would be devastated. He couldn't face going home with the bad news. Instead, he turned Paint toward the McDuffs.

When they came to the fork in the road, Albert expected Paint to trot down the McDuffs' track without any guidance. She loved visiting Magnus and normally needed no encouragement. So he was surprised when she made no effort to turn. He yanked at the left rein, pulling her head around. She yanked back, poking her nose in the air and chomping on the bit. Albert slapped the reins on her rump and she surged down the track at a fast trot, neighing at the top of her lungs, the empty wagon banging along behind her.

Hamish came out of the barn. "Hello, my bonnie girl," Hamish said. "It looks like you're keen to see Magnus." He tried to stroke the mare's neck, but she tossed her head and chomped at the bit.

"It's not Magnus she wants," Albert explained. "It's that foal of hers. It's the first time they've been separated. Paint wants to go home. But I don't!"

Paint continued neighing loudly, forcing both men to raise their voices to hear each other.

"Have you and Margaret had words?" Hamish shouted.

"Not yet, but we will — as soon as I tell her the price I got for the wheat."

"Not much?"

Paint's entire body was trembling with her calls.

Albert yelled to make himself heard over the din. "Not enough to build a house. Margaret won't stay here, not if she has to live in the soddie for another winter."

"She'd be happier if she saw more of Jeanie," the Scotsman bellowed. "It's the isolation that gets to the women, not having anyone to talk to."

It occurred to Albert that both Tommy and Margaret were stronger now and should be able to make the trek to the McDuffs more quickly. But it was still a long way. When the days were short they had to head back home almost as soon as they arrived.

Paint pawed at the ground and let out another deafening round of whinnies. "You could come one day and go home the next!" Hamish yelled. "Jeanie's been saving chicken feathers to make us a feather bed. You can use that! Or we can stuff hay into sewn-up bedsheets."

Albert felt the weight start to lift from him. "You know, I think that might make a world of difference to Margaret. Tommy, too. As you say, it's the isolation. I can't thank you enough, Hamish."

"No thanks are needed, my friend. The offer is a selfish one: we can nae lose you. Now, take that wee mare of yours home before she bursts my eardrums."

With her head turned toward home, Paint's maternal instinct overpowered the respect she had for Albert. She tugged the reins from his hands and took off at a gallop, ignoring his *whoas* and *steady girls*. Egged on by the rattling wagon, she was soon sliding to a halt against the paddock fence, touching noses with her colt and nickering softly. Albert unhitched the mare as quickly as he could and released her into the paddock. Immediately, Maple Leaf butted Paint's udder and started sucking. The mare relaxed, sweat rising from her body in a cloud of steam.

With mother and foal reunited, and Tommy happily watching them, Albert tried to give Margaret an optimistic version of the day's events. She took the news better than he had expected, in no small part because of Hamish's invitation to visit frequently. Albert swore on his mother's grave that the upcoming winter would be the last they would spend in the soddie.

After setting aside money for more laying hens, staples such as oats and beans, thick clothes, winter boots, blankets, and fuel for the stove, they placed some rolled-up bills in a Mason jar labelled EMER-GENCIES. The remainder went in a jar labelled ROOF. They told each other that the roof money was not to be spent under any circumstances. But shortly after, they agreed to use some of it to buy a cow.

It was a good decision. Margaret couldn't stop smiling when she milked the Jersey, or when she watched Tommy drink the creamy, warm milk. She felt sure it would help him grow healthy and strong. She churned cream into butter, and made cottage cheese. There was so much leftover whey and sur-plus milk that Albert bought a piglet so there would be no waste. Tommy got the idea to put the piglet on a rope and walk it like a dog.

"Don't get attached to it," Margaret warned. "That pig is going to be our salt pork. It's not a pet."

"Pigs make good plows, too," Albert added. "Now we've got most of the vegetables out of the garden, you can take him there, Tommy, and let him plow it up for us. But keep a tight hold on him. We don't want him rooting up the winter cabbages … or escaping."

Tommy clutched the rope while the little pig rooted through the ground. It stuck its nose deep, tunnelled through it, and flipped it over. Tommy couldn't help but laugh at the dirty-faced little creature, wiggling its curly tail while grunting and oinking in obvious delight. Despite his mother's warnings, Tommy was getting attached.

But as the pig grew, it became more ornery. One day, it yanked Tommy across the vegetable garden, knocking him off his feet. Valiantly hanging onto the rope, Tommy was dragged face first along the ground until the pig came to a stop at the winter cabbages. It trampled and devoured several before Albert was able to yank the squealing animal to the makeshift pigsty, where it stayed for the remainder of its life.

The family went into their second winter better prepared than their first. They were tougher, fitter, stronger, and they knew what to expect. Paint and her colt were ready, too. They had plenty of hay and a shelter open to the south. Maple Leaf was not afraid to stand in the shelter as his mother had always been. Even when hail struck the roof, he stayed inside, dry and warm. Paint, on the other hand, was conflicted. Maternal instinct told her to remain close to her foal, yet survival instinct told her to flee to safety under the sky. It didn't take too long before maternal instinct won.

As the days became shorter, the hens stopped laying. By December the hungry birds were devouring grain, yet producing no eggs in return. Albert slaughtered one and they cooked it slowly on top of the woodstove until the meat fell off the bones. Keeping track of the days of the week with a fresh supply of pencils, the Coopers reverted to their English tradition of eating a special dinner on Sundays, until all the hens were gone.

As the winter wore on, treks to the McDuffs' house lifted Margaret's spirits. The hours she spent with Jeanie were filled with laughter as well as tears. Both helped Margaret soldier on with surprising fortitude. She was learning to make do with what they had and not complain about what they didn't. She was learning that homesteading was a family affair, and that a man could not shoulder the burden alone. She tried to be more like Jeanie, but always at the back of her mind was the knowledge that somewhere along the homesteading path, this warm, compassionate, and helpful woman had lost her most precious possessions — her two small sons, washed away when the spring thaw had turned the creek into a raging torrent. Margaret was terrified of a similar fate befalling her family.

As the winter deepened and the time drew closer to spring calving, the cow's milk production dwindled. Margaret wondered if it was worth her while braving the cold each day to milk the animal. She decided that as long as she could get even half a mug of milk for Tommy, she would persist. There was no milk for the pig, however, so Albert slaughtered it. The family salted some meat to preserve it, and took the remainder over to the McDuffs.

By spring, all of the chicken and pork along with the preserved vegetables from the garden had gone. The Coopers were once again living on porridge and bannock. This time, however, those meagre rations were supplemented with dairy produce. The cow had calved and was producing gallons of fresh milk.

As soon as the ground thawed, Albert and Paint threw themselves into the work of their second spring on the Canadian prairie. Albert wanted to bring more land under the plow, knowing that more plowed land meant more wheat and more profit to make Margaret's house a reality. Day after day, Paint leaned into the collar with all her strength, pulling the plow through virgin grassland. And Maple Leaf frolicked alongside. He stopped from time to time to snatch a few mouthfuls of grass, then, realizing his mother had moved on, he would squeal, buck, and gallop after her, greeting her again as if he hadn't seen her for weeks.

While Albert plowed, Tommy and Margaret worked in the vegetable garden. Margaret was stunned by the transformation in her son. He had grown taller, but it was more than that. He was both strong and willing. He handled the garden fork with the skill of an adult, and at barely seven he was taking much of the field work from Margaret's tired hands.

As soon as the wheat and vegetables were planted, the Coopers started building the house. It was to be a small, single-storey rectangle that they planned to extend when they had more money. With lots of advice from the McDuffs, and much anticipation, they laid the foundation. Albert was strong and willing, but he had no idea how to arrange the irregularly shaped stones into straight courses. Margaret was only marginally better. But Tommy seemed to know by instinct which stone should be selected from the pile and how it should be oriented to minimize gaps and to create an overall pleasing effect to the eye. Both parents hefted the stones into the position that the boy determined. They started calling him *Boss*. Pride glowed on his sweating face.

Watching Margaret work, Albert contemplated how different she had become from the woman who had travelled with him from England. Her arms were muscled and her back was strong. Her hair was so dry and bleached from the sun and wind that it resembled the parched prairie grass after it had set seed. Pale skin that had burned and blistered during the first summer was now a ruddy brown, but around her blue eyes many small creases had formed from constantly squinting at the sun. Her lips were cracked. Her hands were callused. Her dirt-filled nails were split. And her two dresses hung from her like potato sacks. Yet, in Albert's eyes, she was beautiful.

She was right all those months ago when she told him that owning land had never been her dream. It was his. She had made sacrifices for him. And he loved her for it. But he didn't know how much longer she could go on. He had to get the house finished before winter.

As summer progressed, the walls of the house gradually grew higher. All they needed was money for a roof — *a lot of money*.

"As soon as the harvest comes in," Albert repeated.

Albert was pleased but nervous when he went to town to sell the grain. All across North America, he was told, grassland was being transformed into wheat: the virgin soil was fertile; homesteaders were producing bumper harvests. It was the same old line — supply and demand. Albert was always on the wrong side of the equation.

He couldn't face going home without the lumber and metal sheeting they needed, so he went to the bank. He knew well the risk if he defaulted on the payments, but he considered the chance slight, barely a possibility. Each year he was bringing more of his acreage under the plow. Each year his grain production was increasing. He'd be able to make the payments, surely.

Unless there was a total crop failure. And what was the chance of that happening?

Margaret deserved a home.

With help from the McDuffs and a few other neighbours, Albert and Margaret were able to finish the house before winter. Compared to the soddie, their new house was a palace. The bank manager had been keen to lend Albert even more than he had asked for, and he jumped at the chance to make Margaret happy. With the bigger mortgage, he was able to put two bedrooms into the attic, each with its own small window. This left the entire ground floor as an all-purpose kitchen and living area, with lots of light, a stove, and an oven for baking bread.

In readiness for the McDuffs' first visit, Margaret opened the wooden box they had brought from

England and took out an unused tablecloth. It stirred something in Tommy. He had few memories of the old country except for parts of the voyage: watching the land disappear from view; looking until there was nothing left to look at; vomiting on the rolling deck. Now, the sight of the tablecloth with its knife-edged folds and blue flowers embroidered on all four corners took him back in time. He remembered the day he had watched his mother pack it into the box along with the delicate teacups and saucers that he'd never been allowed to use, and his six toy soldiers. He had a vague memory of his surroundings that day: a small room that brought with it a feeling of gloom, damp, and heaviness.

When Hamish and Jeanie arrived and Margaret served tea, the men couldn't get their fingers in the tiny cup handles. Albert complained that he would need at least three refills in order to quench his thirst. Tommy was so afraid that he might drop and break his mother's prized heirloom that his hands shook, rattling the cup against the saucer. And Hamish did a wonderful impersonation of Queen Victoria, extending his pinkie finger and talking with a perfect British accent. Everyone roared with laughter, and finally Margaret agreed that her precious china was of little benefit to a real homesteader.

CHAPTER THIRTY-ONE

Paint's colt grew into a fine, strong horse. In colouring, he resembled his mother, a black-and-white paint. But in all respects, other than coat colour, Maple Leaf resembled his father. He had the arched neck, a characteristic of the Canadian breed, together with a distinctive thick, wavy mane that floated in the breeze. He had a good disposition, too, not as flighty as his mustang mother, and more willing and able to put his back into the field work. Even though he was only half Canadian, he lived up to the motto of the breed — "The Little Iron Horse." Albert could not have hoped for a better working companion.

Since the Coopers had arrived on the prairie, a one-room schoolhouse had been built for the seven children who lived in the rural part of the township. It took Tommy almost an hour to walk there. His attendance was spotty. When the weather was good, he, like the other schoolchildren, had to stay at home and work on the farm. And many winter days were too frigid for a child to walk three miles each way. Margaret was fearful that he would get lost in a blizzard or succumb to frostbite. When there was little or no snow, Tommy rode to school on Paint, leaving her to spend the day with two other horses in the school paddock. Albert rarely worked the old mare now that Maple Leaf was trained, so he was happy for Tommy to ride her to school. Tommy was happy, too. Despite her protruding backbone he loved to feel her warmth under his legs, and he enjoyed her companionship. When the snow was too deep for Paint to get through, Tommy set off down the road on his snowshoes. But despite these obstacles to his schooling, Tommy was farther ahead in his education than either of his parents.

Albert's thoughts were consumed more and more by the debt they owed to the bank. For two consecutive years, a reasonable crop, coupled with a fair wheat price had enabled him to pay down the loan for the roof, making him almost debt-free. It was then that the bank manager had suggested Albert borrow more, this time to build a proper barn. The existing shelter had served its purpose. It was too small to house more livestock, or store more hay and grain. It was preventing Albert from getting ahead. He reflected that Margaret's dream had been fulfilled with the erection of a stone house, but since the day they had decided to leave England, Albert had dreamed of a barn. The bank's offer was too good for him to walk away from, the temptation too great. So he signed the papers and built his barn. But now he felt vulnerable.

Albert had seen a picture in the newspaper in town: the Great Blondin walking the tightrope over Niagara Falls. Everyone was talking about it, giving their opinion on whether the man was very brave, very stupid, or just plain insane. Albert felt as if he was Blondin, balanced precariously on a high wire. He no longer had his feet on solid ground. At any time, he felt he could fall, and the raging river would wash him over the edge and dash him on the rocks. He had his barn. He had cows, pigs and chickens. He had his family. He should have been happy. But he wasn't. Impending doom stole his joy.

The next summer was a bad one for farmers on the prairies. The seed germinated thanks to the moisture from the winter snow and it grew quickly for the first few weeks, but then the soil dried and no rain came. The young plants stopped growing, the bright green leaves soon becoming tinged with yellow. Terror settled in Albert's stomach like a heavy weight. Day after day he watched the sky, but clouds rarely formed and those that did scudded by, releasing little more than a few sprinkles.

Albert had invested so much energy in plowing and seeding, and now that he had mortgaged the farm to raise money to build the barn he knew that if his crop failed it would be disastrous.

Hamish, confident that rain would soon come, tried to reassure Albert. "It always comes ... eventually. The harvest will be poor, but we'll still have one. You and I, we've been doing everything right. We're not harrowing the death out of the soil, like we did in the old country. That made a grand seed-bed, but in this dry, windy place, the soil blows away. I ken there's a lot more down there, though, so it's no matter if we lose a bit. But there's something wrong when we have to breathe it."

Albert had noticed that recently he, too, had been blowing more dirt-filled mucus from his nose.

Hamish continued. "I hear that most folk are plowing straight into the wind and that the furrows go on for miles."

"It's tempting to do that," Albert said. "I don't know what it's like up in Scotland, but plowing English fields is like driving your horse around a postage stamp — always having to turn the corner because of a wall, a fence, a hedge, or a road. It's so much easier to keep going straight."

"Aye, that's the truth, but the wind races down those long furrows with nothing to stop it, picking up the soil and sending it our way."

"That explains a lot," Albert said. "It used to be that when I blew my nose, I got my own soil. But lately I've been blowing out red soil, or black soil! Who knows where it's all coming from!"

All across the prairie that summer, the harvest was scant. Farmers who had benefited from a passing cloudburst cashed in on the high price of wheat caused by short supply and high demand. Albert was not one of them. Despite his best efforts he harvested barely enough wheat to feed the family through the winter and to provide seed for next season's planting. He was unable to meet his payments on the loan.

Everyone hoped the next year would be wetter.

CHAPTER THIRTY-TWO

The following spring, with the land planted and the seedlings thriving in the snow-dampened soil, Albert's spirits were higher. The warm sunshine and the green carpet that rolled over the prairie did his soul good. He knew that this was the year that would make or break his farm, his family. The bank manager was becoming impatient. He'd said that if there was no substantial payment on the loan by harvest time, then things would be out of his hands. Everything depended on a good crop. Everything depended on rain. Albert felt confident it would come.

Albert and Hamish had come to an agreement. They used Maple Leaf and Magnus as a team, borrowing the horses back and forth as they needed them. No one knew Paint's age for sure, but everyone agreed that she was well into her mid-twenties. Her back sagged, her teeth were worn, and the black patches of her coat were peppered with white hairs. She didn't pull the wagon or the plow anymore. Tommy didn't even ride Paint these days. He complained that her back was too bony.

When Hamish came that morning to borrow Maple Leaf for the day, Paint tried to push through the gate to go with them. She was slower than she had been in her youth, but her survival instinct was still strong. She knew a predator was close by. She couldn't see it, or smell it, but she could feel it. She wanted to run, to get away.

"What's up with her today?" Hamish asked Albert, closing the gate in Paint's face, then reaching over the rail to stroke her forehead. She wouldn't stand still.

Albert shrugged. "Maybe a butterfly got her spooked."

Hamish hooked Maple Leaf up alongside Magnus in the cart. When Hamish clucked at the pair of horses and drove away, Paint ran back and forth along the fenceline.

Hamish waved back to her. "Keep this up, lassie, and you won't be able to move tomorrow. You'll be as stiff as me when I get out of bed."

Paint screamed. It was a warning call, telling the two horses to stay alert for danger. But they didn't answer her.

"What's got into you, old girl?" Albert asked.

She pushed her head into him more forcefully than she should have.

"Hey, stop that! Are you hungry?"

He threw her some hay and walked away. She grabbed a mouthful, then paced again, stalks falling from her mouth as she moved. Then she nibbled the gate post until a splinter got caught between her teeth, so she turned around and rubbed her tail against the same post.

It was then that she felt the change in the air.

The hair rose on her back. She wanted to escape, but the fence contained her. She tried to push through the unyielding gate. The metal latch bit her.

A bird fell from the sky.

🐎

When Albert noticed the cloud, it was just a fine black ribbon stretched across the plain. His heart raced. Rain!

He worked on with renewed energy, pulling weeds from between the young wheat plants. He felt as if a heavy weight had been lifted from him. He felt lighter. He felt optimistic. The wheat would soon be waving in the prairie winds, and the grain would be ripening. He'd make the mortgage payment. He'd settle the tab at the general store. The family would survive another year.

As Albert raised his head to keep an eye on the approaching storm, he was shocked at how quickly it was moving. The narrow ribbon had already become a thick, dark band speeding toward him, growing taller by the second. Then the top started rolling over, bending at the crest like an enormous ocean wave. For less than a heartbeat he was mesmerized. He had come to this new land by ship, seven years earlier, and the relentless rolling swell was still in his mind. Albert couldn't understand what he was seeing. He was thousands of miles from the sea, and anyway there was nothing clean and fresh about this surf. It was ominous and black. Fear came upon him instantly, as if he was punched in the gut. He ran toward home, frantically calling for Margaret and Tommy, looking in all directions for any sign of them, praying they were safe inside the house. "God, help us."

Hamish's head was down, watching the plowshare turn the weeds underground. He had let this area go fallow, feeling that it needed time to rest from constantly giving him a crop of wheat. He had worked the two horses through the lunch hour and his energy was beginning to fade. He wondered what Jeanie had laid out for him on the kitchen table. Bread and cheese, or maybe ham? Deep in thought and with his stomach growling, he didn't see the dust cloud forming behind him, but Maple Leaf and Magnus knew it was there. They were unsettled. Suddenly, Maple Leaf, the younger and less experienced of the two, began to canter on the spot, trying to rid himself of the plow.

The Scotsman was jolted back from his musings. He knew immediately that something was wrong. Perhaps a wasp had stung Maple Leaf. Hamish tried to calm the young horse with his voice and the rein, but to no avail. The big Belgian was upset, too. Magnus was a dependable horse. He never

PAINT

spooked, and always took things in his stride with quiet acceptance, but with Maple Leaf goading him on, and with his human leader unaware of the danger, instinct told him to flee. Unable to control the unusual feeling, Magnus bolted. The plow jumped out of the ground and skidded along the surface, knocking Hamish off his feet and dragging him. He hung onto the reins, yelling whoa.

The plow hit a rock and brought the horses to an abrupt stop. Hamish, shocked that he was still in one piece, scrambled to his feet. It was only then that he saw the approaching cloud. He knew it wasn't rain, and he knew he couldn't outrun it. His best option was to climb aboard Magnus and gallop. But he had no chance of getting on the big horse without something to stand on. Plus both horses were hitched to the plow. Unhitching them would take time, and Maple Leaf was already frantic, rearing and snorting, trying to get away. It was all Hamish could do to hold the youngster back. Despite the panic that was raging inside, Hamish kept calm for the horses. He unhitched the plow as fast as his hands could manage and set Maple Leaf free.

The wind was picking up, the dust starting to blow. Hamish turned Magnus into it and led him alongside the plow. Magnus braced against the wind, blinking his eyes, the wind whipping his mane. With Maple Leaf running in circles around them, Magnus stood still just long enough for Hamish to scramble onto the plowshare and from there onto his back. Then, with the long reins dragging, and without any urging from Hamish, the big horse galloped for home. With Maple Leaf alongside, they flew across the field, the wind chasing them, dust blowing at their heels.

Jeanie had seen the approaching storm. She was anxiously waiting, hoping, and praying that Hamish would make it back in time. As soon as they appeared on the horizon she ran to the barn and flung open the door. Hamish ducked as the horses charged in, and Jeanie slammed the door, locking it behind them all. And then the dust storm hit.

🐎

Tommy was walking home from school when the flock of birds passed overhead. He had never seen a flock this big, not even when the birds were gathering to migrate at the end of summer. They didn't circle, or stray from their path, or swoop and rise again. They flew as one creature. But some were dropping from the sky, flying, it seemed, until they were exhausted. Flying until they dropped dead!

The flock moved on, leaving scattered corpses in its wake. Suddenly the sky opened up once more, as blue as could be. But on the horizon Tommy saw the bank of thunderclouds. He started to run, excited that the wheat would survive and his father would be able to make the mortgage payment.

For years, his parents had tried to keep their worries from him, but he'd heard their hushed conversations, and he saw the stress on their faces. He knew that they had borrowed money to build the house and barn, and that repaying this debt was the reason his father was always exhausted, always pushing himself to plow more, to seed more, to harvest more. But for several years now there had been little rain and the yields had been low. Even with Tommy helping as much as a grown man, the family produced little to sell. The bank, however, still needed to be paid. His father was always behind on his payments, always renegotiating, always pleading, barely keeping his creditors at bay.

This year, for the first time, all one hundred and sixty acres were cultivated. The family was in a position to cash in on what they'd been told were going to be record prices for the harvest. They just needed rain. And it was on its way!

The band of thunderclouds was broadening, still hugging the horizon like a distant mountain range, but becoming more ominous with every passing second. And then the clouds started rolling toward Tommy. His heart lurched, banging into his ribs with a thud. With a fresh burst of speed, he raced toward home.

The black cloud caught him before he reached the laneway. Blinded by the dust that blew into his eyes, he ducked his head and hid it in the crook of his arm, groping his way forward, bare arms and legs stinging as if he was being bitten by fire-ants. He rolled into a ball on the ground, trying to protect himself from the pain, burying his mouth and nose into his chest and using his arms as protection. He held his breath until he couldn't hold it any longer, but when he did breathe, the dust made him cough and wheeze. He couldn't get enough air into his lungs. He couldn't breathe!

I'm dying! I'm being buried alive! I don't want to die.

He dragged himself along the ground, moving forward to where he remembered the house should be.

"Tommy! Tommy!" Albert screamed.

The boy wanted to reply, but all he could do was make a choking sound. It was enough. Albert grabbed his son, threw him over his shoulder, and ran through the darkness.

In the house, his mother hovered anxiously over him while he coughed up mud. He attempted to open his eyes, but the pain was too sharp. Margaret wiped away the dirt with a wet cloth, and after a while he squinted a little. In the flickering shadows from the coal-oil lamp, Tommy saw tears running down his mother's grimy cheeks, carrying soil away in rivulets. Soon tears were running down his cheeks, too. The pain lessened, but his vision was cloudy. He saw everything through a haze. He rubbed his sore eyes, then realized that the haze was in the air, not in his eyes. Dust was blowing in through cracks in the walls. The cracks were so fine that no one knew they were there, yet dirt puffed through them, like flour bellowing from a baking sieve. And dry soil trickled from the roof, like sand in an egg-timer.

Margaret ripped up an old bed sheet. It was

the same one that had covered the dirt wall of the sodhouse. She soaked the squares in water and used them to cover their noses and mouths. The wind whistled over the house. The dirt pounded into the walls and pelted the roof. The door rattled. The windows shook. It felt as if the whole house might blow away with the family inside. They got into their beds and covered up, wrapping the sheets around their heads. Fine sand fell from the roof and covered them with a layer of dust.

"It will pass soon," Albert said, trying to convince himself as much as the others.

But it didn't pass. And with the sun obliterated there was no way to tell for sure if it was even night or day, but they all agreed that it seemed many hours had passed. It must surely be night. Margaret suggested that they sleep, but she wasn't able to take her own advice. She was scared to close her eyes in case all three of them were buried alive. Tommy couldn't sleep, either. His throat burned, his lungs ached, and his eyes throbbed. The skin on his face hurt, and even his arms and legs stung. He coughed, heaving up more muddy mucus.

Albert was anxious about Hamish and Jeanie. When the storm hit, were they out on the prairie, working with the horses? Did they all make it home in time?

He was troubled, too, about Paint. She was in the paddock. Could a horse survive a dust storm this intense? The family cow was several miles away, running with a bull for breeding. She would have been out in the open, too. What were her chances of survival? There was nothing he could do — except pray.

🐎

An eerie silence woke the Coopers. It was still dark. Albert crept out of bed, feeling for the matches and lighting the lamp. The windows were covered with dirt, so he couldn't even tell if it was night or day. He groped his way to the door and forced it open. Sunlight streamed in, along with a mountain of dirt. Tommy climbed up on it. His feet disappeared and the sand started running down the pile again, settling inside the house. From the top of the mound the view was astonishing. It was a different world from the one that existed the previous day. Nothing was recognizable. Nothing green, or even close to green, existed. The vegetable garden had vanished. It was as if it was never there.

Margaret joined Tommy at the top of the mound and looked around. Her mouth opened in shock. Then her tears started. She collapsed into the sand pile and slithered back into the house. "How will we eat? What will we do?"

Albert helped her up and held her. She clung to him, wailing. "How will we manage now?"

Albert was speechless. Eventually he disentangled himself from Margaret.

"Pull yourself together! See what food we have in the house and rustle up some breakfast. Then we can dig out this mess and clean everything up. Tommy, come with me. Let's check on the animals."

"Paint!" Tommy shrieked, running through the shifting sand toward the back of the barn, to the small paddock where the old horse lived. The sand slowed him, threatening to trip him. The drifts came to his knees in places. Soon he was gasping, and his legs were cramping, and his shoes were filled with so much grit that he thought he would be better off barefoot. He rounded the final corner, anxious to hear the old horse neigh, hoping to see her waiting for him.

She was not there.

Sand stretched as far as the eye could see.

"Perhaps she took cover behind a drift," Tommy said, grasping at straws. "Perhaps she found her way into the barn. She can't be gone! She can't be."

Albert was already at the barn door, but couldn't get in. Drifts blocked his way. "Paint!" he called. "Hey, girl. Are you in there?"

There was no reply. He put an ear against the barn boards, hoping to hear a horse moving around inside. But there was no sound. He struggled through a drift to the barn window, which should have been high on the building. It was at knee level! He scraped the dust off it, making a circle big enough to look through. Paint wasn't inside.

Father and son surveyed the landscape.

"See how the sand has drifted to the top of the fence over there?" Albert pointed. "I reckon old Paint just walked right over the top. She probably went off to visit Magnus like she used to in the old days. She'll come back when she gets hungry."

"We have nothing to feed her," Tommy replied. "The grass is buried."

"She can dig for it," Albert said, grasping for one final ounce of optimism, "like she does in the winter …"

And then he slumped to the ground and cried.

EPILOGUE

Pine Ridge Indian Reservation, South Dakota, 1935

Noisy Horse held the child's hand as they walked to the ridge overlooking the Badlands. For the little girl, it was the first visit to this place; for the old man, it was possibly the last. From the ridge they gazed across the valley to the sandstone peaks and wind-whipped pinnacles, the horizontal bands of rusty red and blue-grey and sandy yellow glowing in the afternoon light. It was silent, apart from the constant moaning of the wind and the scream of a bald eagle riding the thermals high into the sky. They were alone: old Noisy Horse and his granddaughter.

Noisy Horse gazed softly into the distance, awed by the beauty of the Great Spirit's work. The cawing of ravens interrupted his reverie. He looked up and watched the birds circling in the bright blue sky.

"Something is dying in the valley," he said, "maybe a rabbit."

Suddenly he remembered another time when he

had watched ravens wheeling in a sky that had been equally as blue. And his boyhood came rushing back to him.

"When I was young, just a little older than you, I found an orphaned mustang in the grass. I carried her home. She became my horse. I called her Paint."

The old man closed his eyes. The girl wondered if he was nodding off, as he often did, but tears trickled down his weathered cheeks. Soon her curiosity got the better of her and she touched her grandfather's arm. "Tell me about Paint. Where is she now?"

"I don't know," Noisy Horse said, his voice catching in his throat. "Shot by the soldiers, perhaps. But I like to think she escaped and joined a herd of mustangs. I still think about her. I wish I could have protected her that day."

"What day?"

"The day the blue coats came with their guns, burning the village and forcing us to march to this place. They shot the horses — so that we couldn't gallop away. Or wage war! I remember Tika, the boss mare. A soldier shot her. I saw. I heard. But some of the horses bolted. I didn't see Paint. I hope she got away."

"I hope so, too," the little girl said. She had not seen many horses in her young life. The white men who visited the reservation generally arrived in automobiles, but there was one man who came on a horse. The child had no fear of the large animal. She waited until the man said she could touch the horse, then she reached out her hand. When the horse responded by touching her with his soft muzzle the little girl felt her chest grow big and warm.

"The soldiers would not allow us to bring anything," Noisy Horse continued. "Just the clothes on our backs! They rode alongside us, but they made us walk. For a moon or more. Some of us died along the way, because there was little food. But I was young and strong, and I survived the march. When we got here, they said that *this* was our place, the place we must stay. The place *they* had given to us! But there were no buffalo here. Even they would not come."

Noisy Horse spoke quietly, almost reverently, as if not wanting to disturb the sanctity of the way of life he once knew. "I remember the days when great herds of buffalo roamed the plains."

"I've never seen a buffalo," the girl said.

Noisy Horse knew that this was true for all of the young people, but his granddaughter's words tugged at his heart and saddened him.

"When I was your age, our lives depended on them. We cut their meat into strips and dried it, or chopped it and packed it into skins, preserved for use in the winter. When I was your age I helped my mother do these things. The men used the bones to make tools and utensils and weapons, and the women used the hides for clothes, blankets, moccasins, and tipis. The skulls were revered as Great Medicine. There was no waste. We used every part. Even hooves for glue, and sinews for bowstrings and sewing thread.

"When Rain stopped falling from the sky and there was no grass on the plains, the buffalo knew where to go. They followed the Yellowstone River, climbing to higher land and forested places that offered shelter. And we followed them to where Rain fell as snow. To where hot water bubbled from under the earth, and trickled in warm streams through icy banks. We sat around the fire in our tipi, buffalo robes draped over our shoulders, and we listened to the elders tell the old stories. That way our history passed from one generation to the next.

"Some of the buffalo gave their lives so that we could live. And we waited there, buffalo and People, until Rain returned to the plains."

"And then did you go back?" the girl asked.

"Yes. When the buffalo returned to eat the grass, we followed them. But then white men swarmed across the land, shooting the buffalo and leaving them to rot."

"Why?"

"The Big Chief in Washington knew that without buffalo we would die of starvation, or grow weak and be unable to fight. Many of us starved, and many died of the coughing sickness. Others, like my family, were shot by the soldiers. And I was marched here and made to stay."

The girl looked shocked. "Why?"

"Because they wanted our land."

Noisy Horse felt bad. The child was barely six, too young to carry the burden of history. Yet time, he knew, was short. There was much he wanted her to know, but he was loath to speak words that would chase away the innocence of childhood.

He wanted her to know that she came from courageous Lakota people. A people who had fought bravely alongside Crazy Horse, defending the Black Hills from the gold miners. He needed her to know that the Hills had been sacred to her ancestors since time began. And that the Big White Chief had given ownership of the Black Hills to the Lakota, to live in without interference from the white man. That was what the Treaty of Fort Laramie had said.

But Custer, the yellow-haired general, discovered gold in the Black Hills, and soon miners rushed in, ignoring the lines on the treaty map, disregarding the sanctity of the place, desecrating it. It was an insult. So Crazy Horse and his warriors fought to defend our way of life. They killed Custer and his soldiers at Greasy Grass, the place the white men call The Little Bighorn. But the victory was short-lived because the Big White Chief could not bear to let us win. So he sent many more soldiers with many more guns. They killed our women and children as well as our warriors. Custer's last stand became our last stand, too.

The lips of Noisy Horse curled back in disdain, and he spoke his thought aloud. "And the Great White Chief pinned medals to the shirts of the ones who killed our women and children."

The girl looked at him, confused.

"After that, the White Chief drew new lines on

the treaty map, placing the hallowed hills *outside* the Lakota reservation."

Her frown deepened.

Noisy Horse wanted his granddaughter to know these things; to warn her about the deceit and lies of the white chiefs. He wanted her to know how *much* they had stolen with those quick marks of a pen.

He wanted her to feel the outrage that he had felt when The Six Grandfathers' Mountain was blown apart with dynamite, then carved with the heads of four great white chiefs!

He wanted her to know that other sacred places had also been stolen: Wind Cave, and Bear Lodge, too. A smile flickered across his wrinkled face as he remembered the massive rock that the white man called Devils Tower. He could see it now, standing alone on the plain, streaked with the claw marks of the spirit bears that lived there. Suddenly old Noisy Horse was once again a small child, sitting astride a horse, his arms clasped around his father's waist, Touch the Sky's hair flying in the wind.

For a second Noisy Horse could smell his father, and feel his strength. Tears welled in his weary eyes. He fought them back, allowing anger to surface.

"The white chief, Roosevelt, made all our sacred places National Parks!" he blurted out. "Parks for the whole nation. Except for us! Yet all these places are on *our* land. Land that the Fort Laramie Treaty had named as *lawfully* ours — until the white man went back on his word and stole these special places with his pen."

The child was bewildered, her brow furrowed.

Noisy Horse looked at her and sighed, almost apologetically. He wanted her to share his indignation, but what good would that do? She was still so young.

He searched his mind for the right words to say. He wondered if he should take her to the mass grave of the hundreds of Lakota men, women, and children who were senselessly slaughtered by soldiers just a short distance away at Wounded Knee Creek. Perhaps she would share his outrage that the troopers received medals of honour for their part in the slaughter. But there were children in that grave who were younger than her. Noisy Horse closed his lips and remained silent.

In his head, the list of grievances kept growing, but he could not make the words come from his mouth. Yet a voice inside him said, if not now, then when? The child would soon leave the reservation and go away to school. Some children never returned. Others came back changed, scornful of the old ways, their heads filled with the white man's language and the white man's ways. They no longer wanted to listen to the elders. As for Noisy Horse, his body still clung resolutely to life, but his spirit yearned to pass on. There was little time for either of them.

He wanted her to know that although the white man had stolen everything from him: his family, his horse and his land, his pride still remained. It was battered and bruised, but it was still alive. He wanted to pass her that spark before it was too late. And, more than anything, Noisy Horse longed to give the child hope in a hopeless world, and a reason to live when all around her there were reasons not to. And this compelled him to speak.

"Granddaughter, listen well and remember — for one day *you* will be the bearer of our history, *you* will be the teacher of the Great Spirit's lessons."

He held the girl's chin gently in his gnarled hand and looked into her clear brown eyes. He knew the weight of the burden he was placing on her slight shoulders. He had carried it himself.

"From the time white men came to this land, they have waged war against us, and against Mother Earth. She did not suffer silently. She tried to show them the error of their ways. At first she spoke gently, but the white men did not listen. So she spoke louder. The white men still did not hear."

The little girl stared, uncomprehending, into the craggy face of her grandfather.

"In school they will teach you the white man's way," Noisy Horse continued. "They will say that *his* way is the better way, the only way. I want you to know that is not true."

The child was confident in her reply. "Then I shall tell the teacher that he is wrong."

"No!" Noisy Horse exclaimed. "They will punish you! You must not speak of these things to the white men. Ever! Promise me, you will not let those words pass your lips."

"I promise."

Noisy Horse was relieved. "In school they will tell you that we are a savage people; stupid and dumb. That is not true, either. For it is the white man who refuses to learn the lessons of Mother Earth.

"Granddaughter, I know that you are young and that you will not remember much of what I tell you today. But commit this one thing to your memory, and hold it safely in your heart until the day your heart stops beating: We are Oglála! Oglála Lakota! And we are a great people!"

She solemnly repeated his words.

"After all these years," Noisy Horse continued, "I still do not understand how the white man could take land that belonged to the Great Spirit, land that the Great Spirit told us to care for. But they did! After they killed the buffalo and put us on the reservation, the white men grazed cattle on our land. Cattle are good to eat, as good as buffalo, but when we left the reservation to kill them, in order to feed our families, the white men killed us, or put us in jail."

"Jail is a bad place, right, Grandfather?"

"Yes. We were accustomed to the sky over our heads, and wide open spaces around us. The threat of jail kept most of us on the reservation, eating the scant rations that they gave us.

"They told us that our hunting way of life was gone, that they would teach us how to become farmers, like them, so that we could feed ourselves and never go hungry. But they gave us only hand tools: shovels and hoes. Not horses and plows like the white farmers used."

"Why didn't they give us horses and plows?"

"Their chief wanted our lives to be hard. He wanted us to remain hungry and weak, so that we would never again be the independent people that we once were. He wanted to make sure we would never be strong enough to take back what was rightfully ours."

"That was mean," the child said.

"Yes, it was," Noisy Horse answered.

"Granddaughter, the Great Spirit makes himself known to us in nature. If we watch and listen we can learn His lessons. But it seems to me that the white chiefs do not hear the Great Spirit's voice. They did not hear, even when the cattle died of thirst and starvation, or when they froze to death."

The girl was confused. "What was the Great Spirit telling them?"

"That severe drought and cruel cold are both a natural part of life on the plains. Our people could have told the white man this, if he had asked. But he didn't ask. He saw that the grassland fed millions of buffalo, so he thought it would feed his cows. But cows are smaller and weaker than buffalo. They cannot thrash their heads to move the snow from the grass. And they were trapped behind wire fences, so they could not roam to search for grass and water and shelter."

"Poor things."

"Some of the white ranchers learned the Great Spirit's lesson," Noisy Horse continued. "They left the land and went away. But the white Chiefs did not learn. They should have given the land back to our people and the buffalo. But they didn't! When Rain returned, they gave our land away again; this time to homesteaders who spoke different languages, but all of them called us savages. And they all agreed with the Big Chief in Washington that we must stay on the reservation because it was the land *they* had given to *us*.

"Like the ranchers, the homesteaders knew nothing about the plains. They brought horses that were as strong as several mustangs, and plows with shares made of metal. And year after year they ripped and yanked and turned the roots of the wild prairie grasses upside down. Wind dried the roots and Sun bleached them. Then the homesteaders grew wheat, which sucked the life from Mother Earth. They loaded that life into wagons and drove it far away."

"Did Mother Earth die?" the girl asked.

"Almost. When Rain stopped falling, as she does once or twice in the lifetime of every man, there were no deep roots to hold down Mother Earth. Then Wind blew from the mountains, as she often does. She worried the bare soil, lifting it in spirals as high as the clouds. Like the ranchers before them, many of the homesteaders learned the Great Spirit's lesson. They abandoned the land that they had thought was theirs, leaving the soil to blow. But deep underground, beyond where the plowshare had dug, some of the grass roots had remained. They were as deep as the height of a woman, and were so entwined with Mother Earth that they did not die. They slept. And when Rain returned, they awoke and pushed green shoots above ground."

"Mother Earth got well again!" the girl exclaimed.

"Yes. She recovered."

"And the Big Chief learned the lesson, right, grandfather?"

Noisy Horse sighed deeply. "No! More homesteaders came, claiming our ancient land as theirs. They did not come with horses and plows, as the earlier generation had. They came with tractors that drank gasoline. A man and a horse could do only so much damage to the earth before they tired. They had to eat and drink and sleep at night. But the tractors never got weary, they never had to sleep. Drivers switched on the lights, filled up the tanks, and took turns. Small tractors were soon replaced by big tractors that moved side by side, ten in a gang, each one pulling a plow, or a harrow, a seeder, or a combine harvester that was as wide as three men, head to toe.

"Day and night, year after year, the machines lumbered across the land like a family of monsters, mile upon mile, acre after acre.

"They plowed the grassland until there was none left. They plowed deeper furrows. They plowed longer furrows. And they went back and forth, breaking the clumps of soil into even smaller pieces, until it was as fine as dust.

"They even plowed the sacred places where our ancestors rested, turning the bones of our people into wheat.

"Mother Earth gave all she had. The wheat she bore was taken away. They gave her nothing in return. Mother Earth grew tired.

"Then after thirty years Rain stopped falling, again.

"All over the Great Plains soil lifted and swirled and blew high into the clouds, and the clouds swept across the land in red blizzards, and black blizzards, and brown blizzards. And the Great Spirit told Wind to carry the soil in her arms across this vast country, and let it fall from the sky on the head of the Big Chief in Washington. The Great Spirit wanted the Big Chief to see what white men had done in their stupidity and their greed. The Great Spirit wanted him to see that Mother Earth was dying.

"Did he see?"

"Yes, he saw. Everyone saw. Even those who lived by the Big Sea."

"And he learned the lesson, right?"

Noisy Horse sighed. "I don't know."

In his mind, Noisy Horse was a boy again. As clearly as if it was yesterday, he watched the herd's boss mare, Tika, extend her neck, flatten her ears, and charge at Paint, ordering the black-and-white filly to get out of her way. Paint tucked her tail and scooted away. The old man smiled at the memory.

And then he heard his father's voice: *There is always a boss mare in the herd. She demands obedience and respect, but in return she protects the herd. She is constantly alert for danger, telling the horses when to run for their lives. They can relax, knowing that she will keep them safe. But they obey her only if they trust her, if they know that she is a worthy leader. Once a boss mare is too old, or too weak, the horses no longer follow her. If she lets them down, they choose a new leader, one who is more trustworthy.*

"I have learned that the white man is not a trustworthy leader," Noisy Horse said.

The little girl chewed her lip, a frown wrinkling her young brow. "Then we must not follow in his footsteps."

TERMINOLOGY

I use the popular term *buffalo* in this book. However, the animals that once grazed the Great Plains of North America are American Bison. True buffalo are found in South Asia and Africa.

I call the People in this story *Lakota*, rather than *Sioux*, as this was the way that they would have referred to themselves in that era. The Oglála Lakota, also known as the Oglála Sioux, are a sub-tribe of the Lakota people who make up the Great Sioux Nation. The Oglála are now a federally recognized tribe whose official title is the Oglála Sioux Tribe of the Pine Ridge Reservation. Notable Oglála leaders include American Horse, Crazy Horse, and Red Cloud.

I use the word *Saskatchewan* to describe the location for the homesteading section of this book. However, Saskatchewan was not designated a province, or named as such, until 1905. Prior to that date, southern Saskatchewan was known as Assiniboia, a regional administrative district of Canada's North-West Territories.

THE MUSTANG

In this story I refer to the mustangs as *wild* horses. The English word *mustang* comes from the Mexican-Spanish word meaning "stray livestock animal." The first mustangs indeed did descend from domesticated animals brought to Mexico and Florida by the Spaniards. Most of these horses were of Andalusian, Arabian, and Barb ancestry. Some escaped and they rapidly spread throughout western North America, surviving without help from mankind for many generations. These are the true wild horses, or mustangs. Other horses known as *feral horses* are dependent to a certain extent on humans. They have different bloodlines from the true mustangs. Most of today's herds show signs of interbreeding with either heavy draft horses that were turned loose in an attempt to create work horses, or Thoroughbreds, a process that led in part to the creation of the American Quarter Horse. But in isolated areas, some herds remain true to their original Spanish roots.

By 1900 an estimated two million mustangs roamed the Great Plains. But viewed as a resource that could be captured for military use, or slaughtered for food (especially pet food), the numbers have declined dramatically to approximately thirty thousand in 2010. Since 1971, mustangs have been recognized by the U.S. Congress as "living symbols of the historic and pioneer spirit of the West." As such, they are managed and protected by the Bureau of Land Management. Part of that process involves culling the horses that are on public lands. The animals are rounded up and offered for adoption to the public. The United States closed down horse slaughter facilities in 2007. Aged and un-adopted horses are therefore trucked to Canada for slaughter. Canada is now the largest exporter of horsemeat to Europe and Asia, and has become the end of the road for many of America's unwanted mustangs. This understandably creates public outcry.

On the opposite side of the controversy are the ranchers who graze livestock on the same public lands grazed by mustangs. The ranchers see wild horses as competing with cattle and sheep for grass.

In Canada, the Sable Island and Saskatchewan horses have some protection under the law, but Alberta's herds are still at great risk.

HOMESTEADERS

Dramatic advertising campaigns by the Canadian Commissioner of Immigration led pioneers to believe that Western Canada was blessed with water and fertile soil along with gold, silver, iron, copper, wood, and coal. On the prairie, the reality was very different. The period leading up to the era discussed in this book had been wetter than usual, creating false expectations of land productivity. Settlers knew that rainfall was light, but they were unaware of the extent or severity of the droughts that had always plagued the Great Plains in cycles of approximately forty years. These droughts were recorded in tree-ring data, and in the stories of the Plains Indians, who were the only people to experience them firsthand.

The dust storms of the 1890s featured in this story were, for individual homesteaders and ranchers, just as devastating as the 1930s Dust Bowl immortalized in John Steinbeck's novel *The Grapes of Wrath*. In both catastrophes, many farmers lost everything when the banks foreclosed on their mortgages. Some moved to the cities and found work, but by the "Dirty Thirties," the decade named for the blowing topsoil, North America was mired in the Great Depression. Jobs were few and far between.

Canada's *numbered treaties*, signed between 1871 and 1921, took large tracts of land away from Aboriginal people, setting them aside for white settlement. In exchange for the land, Canada promised to provide cash, blankets, tools, farming supplies, and so on. The *Dominion Lands Act* began to subdivide these newly acquired Indian lands in anticipation of settlement. And the North-West Mounted Police (NWMP), forerunner of the Royal Canadian Mounted Police (RCMP), maintained law and order during the transition.

The Canadian Homestead Law, almost identical to the earlier American Homestead Act, offered plots of 160 acres to white settlers for nothing more than the filing fee. Applicants received title to the land if they turned a certain percentage of it into farmland within three years, and if they lived on the land for at least six months of each of those first three years.

TIMELINE

Note: *Italic type denotes fictional events in the novel.* Regular type describes actual historic events that support the story.

1858
Noisy Horse of the Oglála Lakota People of the Great Sioux Nation is born.

1868
Treaty of Fort Laramie grants the Lakota Sioux and their northern Cheyenne allies a reservation, including the Black Hills in Dakota and a large area of unceded territory in what will later become Montana and Wyoming. This reservation is for the exclusive use of the Indians. Whites, except for government officials, are forbidden to trespass. Red Cloud, of the Oglála, moves his people to the new Sioux reservation, expecting to receive the food and supplies that the treaties promised. But many Lakota, including Crazy Horse of the Oglála, stay far from the agencies, in the Powder River country of

southern Montana and northern Wyoming. Instead of accepting the government food and supplies, they continue to hunt buffalo. The treaty vaguely allows for this.

1870

Paint is born. Noisy Horse is twelve years old.

1874

Gold is discovered in the Black Hills. White miners flock to the area. The United States government attempts to buy the Black Hills from the Sioux, and orders all bands of Lakota and Cheyenne to come to the Indian agencies on the reservation to negotiate the sale. A few bands do not comply.

1875

Indian agents are directed to order off-reservation Indians to report to their agencies. When only a few comply, the matter is turned over to the military and the course is set for violent conflict.

Paint's first buffalo hunt. She is five years old. Noisy Horse is seventeen.

1876

(February) The United States military starts a winter campaign against the hostiles.

(March) Crazy Horse and his people refuse to go to the reservation. Troops attack their camp on Powder River.

(June 25–26) The Battle of Greasy Grass, also known

as the Battle of the Little Bighorn, or Custer's Last Stand. Angry over gold miners invading their sacred Black Hills in direct violation of the 1868 Fort Laramie treaty, Sioux, Cheyenne, and Arapaho join forces and crush the U.S. Seventh Cavalry, including General Custer's battalion. Custer's death is a humiliating loss for the military.

1877
The U.S. government confiscates the Black Hills by redrawing the boundary lines of the Fort Laramie treaty, placing the Black Hills outside the reservation, and therefore open to white settlement and gold mining.

1877
Soldiers attack the Lakota village. Paint escapes and is caught by Abe, a buffalo hunter.

1880
The buffalo are mostly gone and with them the traditional way of life for the Plains Indians.

1882
Abe gives up his buffalo-hunting business. Paint is sold to Jeb, a cattle rancher who has claimed a tract of Indian land. Paint is twelve years old.

1883
"Buffalo Bill's Wild West Show" is created by William F. Cody.

1886

Summer drought hits the Great Plains. This is
the beginning of a ten-year-long dry spell, part of
the approximately forty-year cycle of drought on the
Plains. This time the effect on the land is worsened
by plowing and overgrazing.

1886–87

Worst winter in living memory, especially in the cattle ranching areas of the Western Plains.

1887

Continuing summer drought puts Jeb out of business.
Paint is sent north to Canada where drought is less
severe and where pioneers need horses.
Homesteaders Albert and Margaret arrive in
Saskatchewan. They buy Paint. She is now seventeen
years old.

1890

Wounded Knee massacre, South Dakota: Three hundred Lakota men, women, and children on the Pine
Ridge Reservation are shot by the Seventh Cavalry.
This is widely thought to be a retaliatory strike after
the crippling defeat suffered by the Seventh at the
Battle of the Little Bighorn. Twenty troopers receive
the Congressional Medal of Honour for their gallantry
in action. These medals have never been rescinded.

1895

Saskatchewan dust storm. Paint is twenty-five years old.

1905
Saskatchewan is designated a province. Before this, it was part of the North-West Territories, District of Assiniboia.

1930–1939
This was the decade known as the "Dirty Thirties." It's been forty years since Paint was lost in the Saskatchewan dust storm. During these years, farming has become more intensive and more mechanized. Horses have been replaced by machinery that needs no rest. With headlamps ablaze, gangs of tractors race across the Prairies, plowing, planting, and harvesting wheat. When severe drought returns, the crops die. With no roots to hold down the soil and nothing to break the wind, the stage is set for environmental disaster. Loose soil begins to blow. Clouds of fine dust, whipped to a height of ten thousand feet, blacken the sky as far as the East Coast of North America and create black blizzards that turn America's "bread basket" into the Dust Bowl. Much of the soil from the Plains is eventually deposited in the Atlantic Ocean. The Dust Bowl is still considered to be one of the most disastrous ecological events in United States history.

1935
Pine Ridge Indian Reservation, South Dakota. Noisy Horse is seventy-seven.

1939

John Steinbeck's book *The Grapes of Wrath* is published, telling the story of a family who is forced from their land by the Dust Bowl and the accompanying Great Depression.

1979

The United States Court of Claims rules that the 1877 Act that seized the Black Hills from the Sioux is a violation of the U.S. Fifth Amendment.

2014

To this day, ownership of the Black Hills remains the subject of a legal dispute between the U.S. government and the Sioux. The land of the Black Hills is home to six national parks: Mount Rushmore, Badlands, Devils Tower, Jewel Cave, Wind Cave, and Minuteman Missile National Historic Site.

ACKNOWLEDGEMENTS

I would like to extend my deepest gratitude to Feroze Mohammed for his guidance with the writing process and continual help with editing, and for making me a better writer.

I also want to thank Jane Warren, my Number One reader; Kate Bowen, my ideas person and sounding board; Tracy Bush, my horse training guru; Rick Revelle, Rob Her Many Horses and his daughters Logan and Devynn for checking the Lakota content of the story; Frank Best, Betty Scuse, Jennifer Scuse, Robert Lawrence, Gail Aziz, and Alice Kong for reading manuscripts; Kimberly Howard and Stephen Lang for photographic and video help; publicist Jim Hatch for his patience with my constant questions; Allison Hirst, my editor; and Allister Thompson, who got the ball rolling with my writing career.

And last, but most importantly, my children, for their love and support: Joanna, James, Erin, Kate, Tarik, and Matthew. I love you.